The Huntress

Diane de Poitiers

Amethyst Gray

ISBN-13: 978-1-9162128-0-0 (Paperback)
ISBN-13: 978-1-9162128-1-7 (Hardback)

Cover design by: Tiras Verey

In loving memory of Carol.

Contents

Foreword

It was Diane de Poitiers herself who quite literally introduced me to Amethyst Gray. After publishing my book about her, Ms Gray and I became friends, with a common interest in this fascinating woman who lived 500 years ago but who still captures the imagination.

This past summer, Ms Gray and I met for dinner in Toronto, where she presented me with the manuscript to The Huntress. I was honoured beyond words when she asked me to write the forward to her novel.

The Huntress is a fresh take on Diane's story, set in the present with frequent flashbacks to Renaissance France and the court of Henri II and Diane's life before she became the mistress of the King. The novel is the first of a series featuring the main character, Diana Garry, and I look forward to reading Ms Gray's future work.

In the meantime, sit back, relax, and enjoy The Huntress!

Shari (Beck) Grenier
Author of "A Portrait in Black and White"

Prologue

You only live once, so you make the most of it if you can. You strive to be the best version of yourself that you can be.

That was how Doctor Diana Garry had been brought up.

It was unashamedly part of her makeup.

It had led her to a first-class degree in Archaeology followed by a doctorate in Roman and Celtic artefacts with a subsidiary topic of Phoenician finds in the Mediterranean. All at Bath Sulis University in South West England.

In late 16th Century France, at the Château of Anet, Diane de Poitiers spoke her last words. "We will be together again Mon Coeur Henri."

I - The Bracelet

"Unbelievable!" Diana Garry exclaimed. It had been a typical morning up until that point. Breakfast at the local patisserie. Strong coffee and two fresh croissants to kick start her day. A staple she had become used to during her time on the dig here in the Loire Valley of France.

Lead archaeologist, Dr Diana Garry from Bath Sulis University's Department of Antiquities, was employed to oversee a dig of a suspected Roman temple. As Bath was situated over the Roman city of Aquae Sulis with temples dedicated to Sulis-Minerva, it was not surprising that she had become particularly enthralled by ancient goddess worship. Her father had been a maverick archaeologist in just this area, bringing his obsession home with him by naming his daughters Tara, Aphrodite, and Diana. Diana always felt she had the best of those names since the goddess she was named after was of the moon, something that she always felt drawn to as a young girl, and because her name was a more common girl's name.

Now here amid a Roman-Era temple ruin was an out of place object found in the confirmed Roman pottery layer. After recording and lifting the find, an initial clean-up revealed a black leather bracelet with what appeared to be two rough green glass beads surrounding a crescent moon charm in silver, despite its green covering of Verdigris.

The design of the charm looked late medieval while the

glass beads seemed out of the ordinary. In the marshy ground, the black leather was surprisingly well-preserved. A small snip would be sent off for dating. The cult of Diana had died out long before the middle ages so finding a potential offering of a crescent moon charm with its apparent links to the moon goddess Diana (in Greek, Artemis) was quite intriguing, but also annoying for a Roman-era purist.

The ruins of the temple of Diana had been discovered quite by accident. An estate worker had been replacing the foundation layer of a walled garden a short distance from the Cher river bank when he had brought up a piece of Roman roof tile. The delicate silver glaze had been identified as nearly identical to catalogued parts held in a museum in Paris. They had belonged to the roof of a temple dedicated to the goddess Diana elsewhere in France. The silver hue was evidence of a roofed 'lunarium' where the moon goddess' altar was covered by a crescent-shaped roof of silver glazed tiles that were said to shimmer in the moonlight.

As soon as the find was identified, a team of Parisian archaeologists descended on the rural château to survey the site with the latest array of non-invasive geophysics devices. A test pit revealed offerings of Roman lead charms, oil burners and broken pottery consistent with a temple site. The later geophysics results showed that the temple was underneath a large rose border at the river's edge, with possibly more of the site washed away by the action of the river.

Now, in her site office in an outbuilding nearby, Diana stared at the remains of this bracelet. Surely it was a gypsy burial? The gypsies of the middle ages were renowned for their superstitions and knowledge of lost pagan sites. The bracelet must have been buried for good luck. And yet there was something strangely familiar about this artefact. Carefully with a small soft brush and tweezers, she was able to get a better look at the glass bead. It wasn't a glass bead as such. It seemed more like a naturally formed droplet of green glass. Diana's young colleague Stanislav Harvel peered over her shoulder. "Moldavite," he said.

"Pardon?" Diana asked, looking round sharply at the tall Czech behind her.

"That looks like a piece of moldavite to me – native to where I grew up in Czechia. My Grandfather and I used to search for them in the fields and lanes sometimes during my summer holidays," continued Stan.

"Oh Stan, suppose you are right? How did a piece of Czech stone find its way along with a lunar charm on to a bracelet that was buried in late medieval times in the ruin of a Roman temple?"

Stan shrugged as he replied. "I must confess that I do not know. But if it is moldavite – and I would say it is from the patterns – then I can only suggest royalty."

"Royalty? In the Middle Ages? I don't need this. We are doing a ROMAN dig. A temple of Diana in the grounds of the château of Chenonceau. I am a Roman specialist – this isn't my field. You studied the Middle Ages – you tell me," Diana protested.

"Perhaps not the Middle Ages. Do you know who once owned this château? A royal in the Renaissance," Stan interjected.

"I do not see how Queen Catherine de Medici fits into this. It is outside of the immediate grounds and outside of her era," Dr Garry insisted.

"Not Catherine de Medici. Before she owned Chenonceau, the château was owned by Diane de Poitiers. The mistress of the King. She revived the cult of Diana in the Renaissance," Stan pointed out.

Diana was stunned into silence. It did make some sense. But the chances of that Diane being linked to the charm or the

Roman temple were remote, surely?

"Maybe. I was given a brief tour of the château when I arrived. But she wasn't royal. Just a mistress," Diana said quietly as if to herself.

"She could have been Queen, she wanted to be Queen, and she acted like the Queen. In all but name. She had access to the royal jewels, she was feted with royalty, and she was symbolised with a crescent moon – three interwoven to be more precise," Stanislav told her.

"Enough speculation. Let's get some analysis done before we go off on a tangent. How are you doing with the roof tiles?" Diana asked, quickly changing the subject.

"Pretty well. It looks like the lunarium is more or less complete, but collapsed, beneath the turf," Stanislav replied, his colleague's change of subject welcomed.

"Good – let's complete the site plan of that area then e-mail it to Paris." Diana relaxed as she spoke.

II - A Dream

That night Diana fell into a troubled sleep. She awoke around midnight and opened the faded brown tapestry curtains to give her a clear view of the château. Bathed in the moonlight across the valley from the guest house it made quite a sight. A wild deer ran across her field of view as an owl swooped low down, hooting as it went. And maybe in the distance gypsy bells were ringing. Or was it a wind chime in the guest house garden?

Diana closed the curtain. Almost before her head hit the pillow, she fell into a deep, deep slumber.

I am a young lady astride a horse wearing a beige and green trimmed riding outfit when I see a woman drowning in the River Seine – on a bend of the river. She has been thrown in from the high steep bank by a group of laughing men up ahead. I am Diane de Poitiers, and I dismount, take off my shoes, climb down the bank, and dive into the river, swim through the cold water out to the woman.

There I take hold of the poor wretch's waist and calming her first I swim with her in my left arm and kick my legs toward the shore – my right arm around the woman's abdomen. There I drag the victim's limp body onto the river bank and up away from the water. We sit there at the river edge until the woman – a gypsy in black clothes – recovers.

Then, holding my horse's reins, we head on foot back towards her camp. En route, the gypsy gives me a crescent moon charm – a small ½ inch flattish charm with a patterned surface of solid, shining silver. She says to me, "This charm will keep you eternally young and beautiful. It will protect you and give you the blessing of the goddess and our beloved Magdalene. I had expected to meet you one day for you are destined for great things. It is yours."

The woman clasps my hand, lets go of it, then enters her camp and nods a goodbye back towards me before she goes out of sight. I ride back to the château of Anet. I keep the charm, put it on a simple but elegant necklace chain and I wear it always afterwards. I mention this experience to nobody.

III - The Gift

Diana's alarm went off. She was somewhat surprised to see her present surroundings. She had almost expected to be in the château. "How extraordinary," she muttered to herself.

She dropped her nightie to the floor and dove straight into the shower. Cold. Refreshing. Reaching for her shampoo, she massaged the substance into her scalp and her dark, shoulder-length brown hair.

Rinsed, clean and refreshed she towel-dried her hair, then patted her tall, slim, muscular frame down.

As a creature of habit, she instinctively put on her black underwear, black t-shirt, black leggings, black socks, and Doc Marten's boots.

Thirty-eight years old and at six feet tall in her flat boots with hair tied back, she presented a striking and commanding figure. She once had a love interest. But on-site Dr Garry was very much the boss. She was dedicated to her profession and could not care less about romance.

Diana was sitting down thoughtfully munching her croissant, sipping at her espresso with her copy of the 'Le Figaro' newspaper in her hand when Stan sat down at the seat opposite.

"The Polish Ambassador is known to have visited the court of Henri II in 1548. He brought a gift of moldavite for the King and 'Madame' – as Diane de Poitiers was known at court." In response to Diana's puzzled look, he continued. "The Jewels yesterday.

Moldavite. 1548 A royal necklace for the King and two matching earrings for Diane de Poitiers – or 'Madame' as she was always addressed."

"OK, but we're not talking earrings," Diana stated.

"Maybe not, but the size is right. And these were a personal gift – not part of the Crown Jewels." Stan stated reflectively.

"I don't follow," Diana admitted.

"Diane had to give back the Crown Jewels after the King died as well as the Château. But a personal gift would stay with Diane. She was meticulous in cataloguing her possessions, and in ensuring she avoided the wrath of the Queen, she ensured every last item went back."

"But why would she have kept them?" Diana pondered.

"She was obsessed with keeping her youthful appearance. Her lover, the King, was 18 years her junior yet at age 58 she could pass for 38. Her body was exhumed a few years ago. It was full of gold. She drank liquid gold as an elixir of youth. The gold eventually poisoned her system and killed her," Stan explained.

"OK – But moldavite?" Diana queried.

"She kept the moldavite as it's also supposed to help keep you youthful. It's the philosopher's stone. It was reserved for royalty for its special powers. It's a fragment of space glass from a meteor that exploded in low Earth orbit and fell to earth in pieces. The glass of heaven. She would have kept it with her, always I am sure," Stanislav went on.

The hairs on the back of Diana's neck stood on end.

"So she would have kept it with her as an eternal youth charm is what you are saying?" Diana realised.

"Yes."

"OK. Yes, but it's speculation to the Nth degree. For all, we know it is glass beads from the Middle Ages buried by a gypsy." Diana gulped as she spoke as the significance of the gypsy in her dream and the burial struck her at that moment.

"Are there any Romany families still living in this area?" She asked.

"Maybe. I can ask. Why?" enquired Stan.

"I fancy getting a tarot reading." Diana smiled mischievously.

"OK?" Stan seemed puzzled.

IV - Mamon

The family of Mamon Mystique had been in the area around Chenonceaux for hundreds of years. Formerly nomadic the Romany clan had finally settled around a small wood to the east of the château. They still maintained some traditions, with a mixture of modern caravans, traditional trailers, and shacks. Being the elder Matriarch with rheumatism in the winter Mamon now stayed in a modest wooden hut at the far end of the camp.

It was to Mamon's shack that Diana Garry now headed to during her lunch break. She wasn't quite sure what she was going to ask, but she knew that this was the place she had to go.

Stan had made the initial arrangements. A labourer employed at the site had turned out to be one of Mamon's grandsons. Over a coffee and a Gauloise, the men had discussed the Romany family's pedigree in the area.

As Diana went to knock on the door to the shack, to her great surprise, the door swung open, and a small, dark lady in a traditional cream crocheted woollen shawl and a rustic costume was standing there.

"Mamon Mystique?"

"Yes, my child. Oh, so beautiful, I have been expecting you for so long. Sit down, *Madame*."

"Madamoiselle. I'm single. Just call me Diana."

"But of course. Such a pity. But maybe not for long now."

"Do you know why I have come to you today?"

"Yes. To discuss your bracelet."

"That is partly true, yes. We have discovered a much later find in amongst our Roman temple remains. The leather carbon dates to between 1500 and 1570. The experts say that the stones are quite unusual."

"Moldavite. The Royal stone from the stars. But you have not mentioned the charm, *Diane*." The Romany stressed the name.

Diana coughed but decided not to correct the old lady.

"The crescent moon charm. That style is said to be from the fifteenth century. So earlier still. Perhaps reuse."

"An heirloom from my clan. My twelfth grandmother possessed it as a child. Her father made it as a good luck charm for her. I believe it saved her life. She nearly drowned, but was saved through an act of kindness, Diane."

Diana shivered, as the old lady mentioned the charm in connection with a near-drowning. Her dream. But how? Surely a coincidence.

"I'm sure that the river can be treacherous around here during the floods and storms," she said.

"Oh no, not the river around here. My very great grandmother lived near Anet. She was thrown in the river Seine by her high-born lover. She was pregnant and left to die. But she was rescued. As you know." The old lady smiled to herself.

Diana did not fall for the bait. It may be coincidental. Anet was far from here.

"No. Please go on."

"A beautiful young lady on horseback came to her aid. My very great grandmother could not swim and nearly breathed her last. But the high-born lady with a heart of goodness pulled her to the bank and made her cough up the river water. She was saved as was her child. All she had of value was her moon charm. But in an instant, she realised that it must be gifted to this lady.

On the way to her father's tent, she pressed the charm into that lady's hand and told her how it would keep her safe and young throughout her long life."

"Amazing," Diana commented.

"That lady was Diane de Poitiers. She later helped my grandmamma's child come here. The child was called Diane in her honour."

"So, Diane de Poitiers is the reason your family came here?" Diana asked.

"Yes. And after Madame died her daughter returned the charm to my foremother Diane. But there was a problem. The charm came along with some other jewels that could not belong to commoners. Queen Catherine owned the château here by then, and my family was fearful of her retribution if she found out. So, it was decided to bury them under the light of a new moon. It was the new moon nearest to mid-Summer 1568. The place of the goddess, just inside the wall of Diane's garden. Kept for safe-keeping until she returned for it."

"Do you know anything of these Royal Jewels?" Diana inquired.

"A little. The jewels were said to be green. I often wondered about them when I was a little girl. It was only later when my grand-daughter bought a moldavite necklace charm that I realised the connection. They were only for royalty in the Middle Ages."

It all fitted.

"Yes. I understand. But how did your foremother know about the Temple to Diana/Artemis?" Diana asked again, intrigued.

"When she arrived at Chenonceaux along with her brother she, and he joined with other Romanies here. Upon her marriage, she was initiated into the local Romany legends and ways. The Temple to Diana was built on a sacred spring that has healing properties at the full moon and new moon. The Celts had a small shrine to the spring there. When the Romans came to the Loire valley, they built temples to all of the elements., so the spring shrine was replaced by the temple to Diana. It stood and prospered for hundreds of years before it was sacked and burnt to the ground as the Roman Empire collapsed. When my people came here, its memory was fading, but we recognised the sacred healing spring and settled nearby. When the village expanded the last of the exposed temple, stones were robbed for building material, and the site was ploughed. But we remembered." The old lady glanced at her visitor, trying to gauge her reaction.

"But why did she bury the bracelet there?" Diana was full of questions, for which she needed answers.

"But of course the bracelet had belonged to Diane de Poitiers. She was born under the sign of the goddess. My people believed she was an aspect of the goddess. She had a magical aura that helped France prosper and kept her young and beautiful. When she died, it was only right that the bracelet was returned to the goddess here."

"I see. It does explain so much. You have been so helpful. Thank you kindly." Diana smiled slightly, trying to show the helpful old lady some warmth and gratitude.

"Diane always lived near to the temples of Diana. I don't know if she knew or not. But her other main home at Anet lies on another temple to Diana. It is near to her tomb and where she is now rightly at rest. She would want you to know *Diane*."

"OK. But one site at a time. I will make enquiries. Thank you very much again for your time."

The women parted company very warmly. Diana returned to the site office to search for other Diana temples in France.

V - Gems

Back at the site office, Diana was waylaid by Stan with two sets of big news. Firstly, a broken porcelain bust of Diana had been found under the collapsed lunarium roof. Pieces of it had been recorded and lifted. Remarkably the lunar crescent on the top of the head of the goddess was still attached and was made of silver. It must have glinted in the moonlight at ceremonies and when lunar observations were made by the Priestess at the temple.

The pieces had been placed in a significant 'finds' tray by Jaques' restoration area. Jaques, a spindly be-spectacled man in his late 20's with ginger hair, was busily brushing and chipping away the dirt on the pieces of the bust. Diana decided not to engage him in conversation. He was a man of few words at the best of times. It was usually better just to leave him alone.

The other piece of news was a great confirmation of Mamon's information. The results had come back for the bracelet.

"The carbon-14 dating indicates that the leather strap dates back between 1480 and 1580, with a luminescence indicating a date closer to 1550." Stan seemed very excited in the tone of his voice.

He continued. "And the spectroscopy on the charm indicates silver, while on both stones it confirms moldavite, originating in Czechia. The Czech King, or rather the Monarch of Bohemia, did not part with the stone very easily. And no peasants were allowed to keep the stones for themselves on pain of death. It was only in the early 16th Century that a territorial dispute with Poland led to a settlement of three pounds of Moldavite being handed to the Polish king. He was much more lavish with his gifts, ingratiating himself with both the Holy Roman Emperor Charles V and Henri II of France."

"The Polish Ambassador's Report mentions the elegance of the French Court in contrast to the drab court of the Emperor. It also mentions the beauty and charm of the King's companion, who he refers to as 'Madame'. Madame's delight was gradually enhanced as the Royal Stones were placed in her hand. Her natural beauty radiated from her face.' 'Madame' was a term for Henri's mistress Diane de Poitiers. I think we have a match. The date of the report was 1552." By the end, Stan was gasping for breath.

"Wow, that's great. Good work, Stan. I should go and speak to the château about this, and get some more background on Diane." Diana was blown away by the new information.

VI - Chenonceau

M. Le Clerc, the Château Manager, was slightly bemused by the sudden call from Dr Garry. What could they possibly have found in the garden that related to the château? Having a Roman temple ruin would bring in more tourists, but it didn't add to the story of the château itself. Surely it was just some old garden waste otherwise.

Jean Le Clerc was a portly man in his early 60's, mid-height with dark features and thinning hair. He had taken the job as manager after retiring from his career as a police inspector. The psychological healing effect of the magnificent château on the banks of the Cher tributary to the Loire with its historic halls, gardens and bedrooms had mellowed him from being a gruff anxious man to a much calmer relaxed and friendly individual. He enjoyed his job and was well thought of by the family who owned the château and the staff who kept it running.

When Diana Garry arrived at his office, Jean had already located the file of the English publications relating to Diane de Poitiers and the Château. His newly published 'History of Chenonceau' guide book, 'A Portrait in Black and White' and 'The Serpent and The Moon' were ready on his desk to lend to Diana.

"Ah, Dr Garry. How nice to see you again. I trust that it is good news you bring?"

"I think so M. Le Clerc."

“Call me Jean.”

“And I Diana. I’m not one for formalities.”

“What is that intriguing package in your hand?”

“I have brought a bracelet that we have good reason to believe belonged to Diane de Poitiers. We have cleaned it up and placed it in a display box, so you can add to your ‘finds’ cabinet if you wish. Here.”

“It is fascinating. Can I get you a coffee?”

“Please – espresso.”

“Here you are.” He handed her the small cup with steaming coffee in it.

“Thank you. The bracelet is both curious and unique. It is a silver crescent moon charm surrounded by two small moldavite gems. The charm is an artisan item while the gems are linked with Royalty. The strap dates to the Renaissance.”

“I see. That is certainly an interesting find. A bracelet that has a moon charm with some Royal stones. It could be Diane de Poitiers’ – but do you have any evidence? We can’t just make random claims.”

“Of course not, Jean. It seems that a gypsy gave Diane a lunar charm when Diane rescued her. This bracelet could contain that charm. It is also likely that Diane was presented with the moldavite stones by the Ambassador of Poland – my colleague has uncovered documentary evidence. Very few people had access to those Royal stones. Similarly, very few people would have had pagan charms in that period. The crescent moon was also Diane’s symbol, I believe.”

“That is incredible. But Diane died at Anet, a long way from here. The charm she is said to have kept with her throughout her life. By her death in 1566 Diane was no longer in residence here.

Her château was taken over by Queen Catherine de Medici after the King's death some years before. So, I do not see how it could have ended up here."

"The local gypsies have a legend that the charm was returned to the daughter of the Romany that Diane rescued. And by then, that woman was living here."

"Magnifique! What an incredible find Diana. And so appropriate that you, her namesake, should have made the discovery. I don't believe that I have shown you around the apartments here. If you can indulge me for a while longer, I will give you a tour around. I also have some books for you in English. And perhaps you should visit Diane's resting place at Anet. I know the proprietor there. He would be pleased to show you around, I'm sure."

"I would be delighted. The dig knows that I'm here if I'm needed."

VII - The Tour

Jean Le Clerc provided Diana with a full tour of the Château. To Diana's great surprise, it seemed very familiar, yet this was her first visit here.

The lower level of the Château above the river has a secret door that leads to a stairway into the river. Jean unlocked the old wooden door and showed the staircase to Diana. As she looked down into the gurgling waters, Jean's voice seemed to disappear, and the view changed.

I am now wearing a bathing robe with a towel in my hand walking down the corridor in the early morning light going down the wide spiral stairs into the Cher river. The water is cold, the air is Autumnal, I swim and float out with the moderate current, into the sheltered edge of the Cher. A mist is rising; there is weak sunlight; the garden has its roses. The wall and silhouettes look peaceful. I push off and swim back to the stairs. Swimming against the current helps to strengthen my left knee, which is feeling weak. It is exhilarating, and I feel alive.

I ascend the stairs again, dry off with the towel, and put on the robe. I go back up to my bedchamber. My maid, Sarah, has my clothes out on the bed for me. I put on plain linen underskirts then a black dress of velvet, embroidered at the top with silver crescent moons, small ¾ inch wide, pointing in different directions, all the way around the bodice. The skirt is plain black. I put on soft black leather slippers.

I sit down on a padded stool with a white/green pattern, with carved legs and out-turned feet, in front of a silver dresser with a vertical oval mirror surrounded by silver metalwork shaped like twisted leaves. There are multiple drawers in two rows. It has a smooth, rounded shape, like the side of a grand piano, so surrounds me slightly as I sit onto it. It has a ceramic jar of duck fat on the dresser. I take some of the duck fat and massage it into my arms and legs.

I take out a silver brush from one of the drawers. It has a wooden head with small brass nails banged into it – about 20-30. The back of the wooden head is covered in silver too. I brush my hair with it for five or so minutes. I sit at the dresser in front of the mirror while combing my hair. Sarah wraps my hair into a sort of a bun at the back and secures it with a whale-bone pin about 2 inches (5 cm) long and 1/5 inch wide (5 mm), it is natural cream bone coloured.

I go downstairs to a small chapel. It is deep recessed but narrow, has high windows with a short stained-glass pattern in the centre of the window. There is a small altar with a silver crucifix in the centre. On the right are a set of three images of Mother Mary (in blue and white), Jesus (in white and brown) and Mary Magdalene (in red and blue with her apothecary bottle). I kneel and pray, crossing myself in the devout Catholic manner. I know Henri is away at war so pray for his safety and kiss the ring he gave to me that is gold with intertwined crescent moons.

After 20 minutes or so I go down to the main hall, but look into the galley/kitchen en route to request my food and say good morning to the servants. I have a cut crystal glass of water poured from a crystal decanter from a nearby special spring that has been brought each day freshly by a servant, a goblet of red wine and a small wooden (turned, round) bowl of autumn berries from the estate. I eat nothing else – I do not have a big appetite.

Afterwards, I summons my clerk – Dominic Du Pré, a small,

round, ratty man with round glasses and a leather beret. We discuss the ledgers - big bound fabric books with hand-written accounts with natural beige colour bindings, thick vellum paper, ruled pages and thick margins on the right-hand side of each page - and the Chenonceau estate. The accounts take about an hour.

The next thing Diana knew was that she was at the Private Chapel, looking transfixed at the plain window. She turned to Jean and asked, "Where is the stained-glass window of Mary Magdalene?"

"Pardon, Mamselle?"

"I'm sorry, but I was expecting to see a different window."

"I'm afraid it was broken during the Terreurs. The whole place could have been destroyed if a later owner had not intervened. We have a sketch in our archives. But how did you know?"

"I don't know. Intuition?" She flushed deep red in her face.

"Fascinating." Jean gave her an intense look into her eyes. She flushed even redder.

The tour continued upstairs.

As Diana looked at a painting on the wall – of Diane de Poitiers as Diana the Huntress – a voice spoke to Diana inside her head. "I am you." Diana became faint and passed out.

I am in the gallery of the château of Chenonceau, lying upon a chaise longue completely naked, my hair braided into a tiara and resting upon a red silk sheet. Opposite me is a male painter, fully dressed in his Renaissance finery, easel in front of him with a paint palette and paintbrush in his hands as he looks intently back at me. I know that I must stay still as he is painting me. I am cold, even though the sun is shining through the windows onto my bare breasts.

"Doctor Garry, Doctor Garry."

"Uh, yes, uh."

"Are you OK, Doctor Garry?"

"I don't know. What happened?"

"You were looking at the painting, and then you just passed out. But luckily you seemed to go down gently and didn't bang your head. Can I fetch you water or some coffee?"

"Ah, yes, perhaps a milky coffee with some sugar. May I sit down for a little?"

"Of course. Here, sit down on this chair."

Jean gestured to an armchair in the corner and moved it out so that Diana could sit on it.

"Will you be OK while I fetch your coffee?"

"I should be. I'll sit quietly and close my eyes."

While Diana sat with her eyes closed, she had another vivid dream.

It is Summer in the Loire valley. It is the first light of dawn. Covering myself before and after in my black cape, I take a vigorous swim in the Cher river, via my secret door from the château. I am now dried and refreshed, wearing my beautiful, light hemp cloth riding dress of black with riding mask to protect my face, when the sun is stronger. I mount astride my big brown horse 'Ermin', and speed off at full gallop along the Cher valley, through the green fields of the flood plain, up to the edge of a large wood with a great oak tree that marks my turning point. I ride back again at break-neck speed.

Now back in the château 'taking my privée' and splashing my face and eyes in a bowl of newly collected spring water before retiring again to bed 'au naturel' for a couple of hours before breakfast.

Now breakfast of summer fruits, some yoghurt, and a small piece of bread with soft cheese. I discuss with my clerk about the estate. Now out relaxing in my garden, smelling the roses, hearing the birds and sitting under my summer house's canopy to enjoy the view – including a new fountain. I feel so relaxed here. As I doze, Henri appears in the garden having just arrived back. It is now early afternoon but even so we retire to my chamber. Although now mature and past child-bearing age I still enjoy lovemaking with Henri.

What did it mean?

When she was a child, she was very fond of her grandfather. He used to sit her on his knee and tell her stories. He would often come over for supper on the weekend and play games with Diana and her sisters. But his favourite was Diana.

As she received her offer of a place at London University to read Archaeology as an undergraduate, she had gone to bed content. While listening to her tape Walkman, she had suddenly had a strange feeling.

"Grandfather." She had turned off her Walkman, looked around her room, then carried on listening.

The next day her Aunt called to say that her Grandfather had passed away suddenly, after seemingly spilling his hot cup of tea on his lap.

After that incident, Diana had begun to wonder if there was an afterlife. But she had never seriously contemplated there being anything after this life. In the west, it is just not taken seriously while in Hindu and Buddhist cultures the idea of reincarnation is widely accepted.

Diana shook her head. "I must be working too hard. How could I possibly be her?"

Diana looked around the magnificent surroundings where she was sitting. The painting seemed so vivid. The room seemed strangely familiar yet unfamiliar. The sort of familiarity she had experienced when visiting her parents' house back in Dorset. These days as she looked over the ruins of Corfe Castle, she noticed the unfamiliar wallpaper in the living room, the new carpet, the adult leather settee, and the gas central heating.

It was a far cry from the crowded room with her dolls' house and her sisters' playthings strewn around. The old settee with the dodgy springs that she and the other two girls had enjoyed jumping on was long gone. Her father's grey hair reminded her that he was now retired from his University post and was now resident archaeologist at the castle they had for so long considered their own.

Could it have been that this beautiful château had belonged to her in a past existence? How could it be? It was charming, but Diana Garry was English. Both of her parents were from the West Country. In a few short years, she would be 40. As a new year began, she had already become a year older herself. She had the added annoyance of getting combined Christmas and birthday presents. She was a normal girl. She must be working too hard.

Her breast heaved as the conflict between her logical brain, and her intuition was fought. This was not the first time. Only a few years earlier she had been invited to observe the excavation of a car park in Leicester. There a woman had pointed to a spot on the tarmac that had been inexplicably marked with an "R". That woman had been convinced that the body of King Richard III of England lay there. Diana's logical brain told her it was impossible, yet her intuitive self knew that the woman was correct.

A short while later a slightly deformed skeleton was discovered under that very spot. Later tests confirmed the identity of the remains. It has been a watershed for Diana too. She realised that trusting her intuition was the way forward. On delving through archaeological reports and contemporary news reports, it was often 'on a hunch' or through 'a feeling' that the most significant discoveries were made.

"Diana, are you OK?" Stan had arrived and was standing in front of her, yet he appeared quite different to her now. He was dressed in elegant breeches; a suede doublet and he sported a handsome beard. "Diane, Diane."

It was a spring-like day in 1536. At the weekend. Early afternoon. At a Château belonging to Anne de Montmorency. I am wearing an elegant and shapely black velvet dress, a lace-up back with black laces, a pinched-in waist below a bodice. There is embroidery on the bodice front and down my skirt to the floor with silver thread and silver 'tufts' all down the front to the ground in a full vertical stripe at the front. It is exquisite. My hair is loose and long, shining gold, a lace basket is keeping my hair together and tidy. There is a strong scent of lavender on me and in the room. It is a fantastic room with cherubs and angels on the ceiling. It has a similar style of large romantic tapestries on the wall. There is a patterned silk cover on the bed – creamy beige with a paisley-like pattern on it. It is a four-poster bed – smart and new. It is open at the top so I can see the mural on the ceiling. There are small marble tiles on the floor. It is a large room. The door is facing the bed with a largish window on the left, on the first or second floor of the château.

I lead Henri in, holding his hand. I say 'Do you find me attractive?' He replies, 'Why yes, of course!'. I kiss him on his lips, his clipped beard tickly on my chin. I place his arms around me and put his hands on to the lacing at the back of my dress. I say 'I'm yours.' My feelings of excitement make me feel a little breathless. He starts to untie me. We kiss while he unties me and I undo his light brown suede jacket with its peg-like buttons. My dress and his jacket both fall to the floor.

I am naked, vulnerable, his. I whisper, 'I have always loved you.' 'Me you also,' he replies. I unbutton the round brown leather buttons of his blouse. He undoes his breeches – three buttons. I then unlace his shorts. We embrace, and I pull him towards the bed. We go onto the bed; we pull back the covers to reveal its black satin sheets. My skin, white like a lily, is a stark contrast to his young tanned body and the black bedclothes.

I caress him, and he touches me. I carefully massage his slightly twisted member then pull it towards and into me. We roll over with him on top, and we make love. It is a moment of joy for him and for me. It is the consummation of our love. We are both ecstatic. The pleasure is all-encompassing. Afterwards, we caress, kiss, hold hands, explore each other, and talk of our love. It is absolute bliss. We lie there for hours and make love again two more times. I never want it to end.

VIII - Dreams

Diana awoke in her room, back in her lodgings. The Sun was setting, and she was still dressed, but she had been tucked into bed. Her shoes and her bag were neatly beside her bed.

She made as if to get up, but her head was throbbing, so she lay back down on her pillow, feeling strangely exhausted. Sleep enveloped her, and she began a series of dreams...

We always address Anne de Beaujeau as 'Madame.' She has a strong jawline. She is elegant but understated. She is calm and rarely raises her voice. She wears beautiful but straightforward gowns in cream generally with minimal jewellery. She always covers her main dress with more layers of cloth in beige and light green. All are made simply from flax. Her hair is mid-dark brown and often covered or platted into a basket. She seems tall and always sits slightly higher than us girls, of which there are around five or six in a group. We girls, with whom she sits, wear simple cream gowns, made of flax again. We are always clean washed with tidy hair. Madame has an appreciation of nature and as often as not holds her classes outside on the lawn. The house is like a manor - a large house with some walled gardens and a moat along with some classical features and is fronted in limestone. It has carved limestone vase-like structures on some corners in the garden. It has very decorative elements despite this being in the early 1510s.

We girls sleep two or three to a bedroom with a shared maid or two maids sleeping on a mat on the floor while we sleep in wide-ish single four-poster beds with beige and brown patterned curtains around us. The beds are a bit hard, but we got used to them after a while.

The food consists of sumptuous dishes that are found at a formal banquet - just not so many of them. Madame teaches us etiquette at the table and even demonstrates to us the correct way that a fine lady should drink her wine from a goblet. I find myself practising lifting the goblets many times as I struggle to grasp the concept for some reason. Madame calmly repeats 'Come on, Diane.' Every moment is considered a lesson but is made enjoyable as much as possible as that is important later on. Lessons include how to steal a man's heart - vital for happy political unions later on. And it is not to be used lightly. Other lessons involve hygiene and beauty tips.

She is strict but fair. If any of us are sent to our room, she comes up later and discusses with us why it had been necessary. She gives wise counsel, is fair and measured. We girls sit on chunky wooden carved bench chairs with low backs while in the garden. There are usually very few men around. The lessons are secluded. There are only male gardeners other than women servants present except when we have visitors. This period feels like a happy time in my life.

The vision lifted and was replaced by another.

I am now aged 15. I am wearing a plain green, but elegant dress in the Medieval style and I am marrying Louis de Brézé, seigneur d'Anet, and Captain of Rouen a man nearly forty years older than me. We are in the main garrison church outside the walls of the crumbling château of Rouen. Louis is the grandson of King Charles VII and serves as a courtier of King Francis I. It is a great honour for me, I am told. But I feel sick with apprehension at waits ahead for me with this old man.

The scene fades and is replaced...

The war with Spain has gone badly, and the King has been

captured and is being ransomed back in exchange for his two eldest sons. For the last leg of the long journey to the border with Spain, I am in a carriage with the King's sister Marguerite and the two princes. The carriage is nicely carved in beechwood but is more functional than luxurious. It has a curved roof but has no glass in the windows. Marguerite is in a yellow dress with gold trim that is relatively light. I am wearing a cream dress in a bright satin material with a green panelled skirt and an embroidered bodice in cream with beige slippers. Prince Henri, seven, and Prince Francis the Dauphin, eight, are in smart suits of tan leather and beige suede, including their breeches. They wear matching squashed hats with feathers, white cream shirts and tan laced boots. Both boys look sullen, Henri is sobbing at times.

At the river, a small crowd has gathered on both sides – but is more abundant on the Spanish side. The river water is green-brown and slow-moving. The Princes are beckoned on to the barge by a French noble. Francis moves directly, but Henri hangs back turns and sobs. At this point, I move towards Henri, kiss his forehead and give him a hug. I tell him "You will be fine. Be brave, my Prince." Henri smiles back at me, then moves to join Francis on the barge.

The barge is full, broad and flat – more like a ferry and large enough to accommodate a cart-horse (but not the cart) with an oarsman on each corner, it is dark stained wood coloured. The barge is loaded with cases of gold and silver in ingots and coins. Ten armed men are flanking the Princes and the cargo. They row out to a pontoon in the middle of the river as the King's barge rows out from the other side. On the Pontoon the King embraces the Princes in turn briefly while the cargo is transferred and checked by the Provosts (Auditors) of both parties standing on the Pontoon.

Anne de Montmorency acts as negotiator so ensures that the transfer goes smoothly. Finally, after some minutes, the King and Anne get on to the French barge as the Princes get on to the other. A curt nod from the King and both head to their respective shores.

The transfers continue with other nobles and the princes' staff and others for some time afterwards.

At the shore, the King, in leather breeches, cream blouse but holding his leather jacket, throws up his arms (as if victorious!) to the waiting crowd. Then after embracing his sister and without further ceremony, he and Anne get onto their waiting horses and ride straight back towards Paris. I am feeling full of apprehension for the fate of the princes and am shocked by the King's almost callous attitude. The King's mistress doesn't appear to be present or at least stays away from the riverside.

The scene changes again.

I have memories of Normandy – clear flat fields full of sheep. Some Norman brown and white cows, but mainly sheep.

Once more, the scene changes.

I am at Rouen Cathedral a few years later. It is 1531. There is a slight chill in the air, but it is sunny for the procession. I am with both of my daughters, who are both shorter than me and are slim. All three of us are veiled in thick black lace, with black dresses with layers of black lace. I am overcome with grief at the loss of my companion and mentor – I have a sense of emptiness, apprehension and fear of the unknown.

I see the Priest and his assistants – the men in white swinging smoking incense containers - with the oak coffin following behind, being carried by six squires in dark colours with purple sashes. My daughters and I follow directly behind as we enter the cathedral through the wide main doors with King Francis I (at the front) and the other nobles slightly separate but behind me.

In the cathedral, my family are seated on the left at the front, but I mainly stand, sometimes sobbing, behind the coffin, its lid off, surrounded by six large candle stands, decorated by cream lilies, as are parts of the cathedral. There is a strong scent of flowers mixed with incense. It is quite light as it is mid-afternoon, but there are still plenty of candles.

Speeches are given – even by the king –, but I am not really 'present' to remember them. The Priest gives the absolution and the blessing (benefactus). I lean forward to kiss Louis' cheek. It is cold and clammy. I place a small poesy across his folded arms. He is wearing a smart outfit with a white shirt but with ribbons representing his stewardship plus his other titles, and a dark jacket. He still appears solid and stocky even in death. The coffin is lead-lined with white lace inners. The lid is closed. The casket is carried to an open vault in the floor and lowered down on ropes by squires and churchmen. I am in tears, as are my daughters.

IX - Trouble

Diana's mobile rang. It woke her up from her deep sleep. It was her mother, Karen Garry. "Darling, how are you?"

"Oh, I'm OK. I think I've had a touch of the 'flu. I must have been overworking. But I've had a deep sleep, and I feel so much better for it."

"That is so good D. That nice assistant of yours, Stanley, called me as he was a bit concerned. Apparently, you passed out on a visit to the Château. It's not like you at all. I hope you are eating enough. You really need a man and some children around to look after you."

Diana sighed. Her mother was priceless. She had managed to turn the conversation from concern for Diana's wellbeing to worry for her own descendants. Diana's two sisters were even less likely to produce children than she was. Tara was in a relationship – but with another woman. And neither of them wanted children. And as for Aphrodite, her string of failed romances were the staple of mother's conversations to family and friends. Somewhere along the way, she had picked up an infection that had probably robbed her of her fertility. In short, Diana was her mother's best hope for grandchildren. And that was why conversations were kept short with her mother. That and nausea she felt whenever she was using her mobile for more than two minutes.

"Mother! I'm thinking of having a hysterectomy as a

precaution."

"No! Since when?"

"Since when you just rang! I'm not settling down. And Stan is 'Stanislav'! He's nearly young enough to be my son, so don't start."

"Don't joke, darling. You know how it hurts mummy so. With Tee and Aff like they are, I'm sure you can see it in your heart to make me a granny?"

"Mother, you are just amazing. You've woken me up to ask how I am, and now you are talking kids again. Please change the record!"

Diana's mother did drop the topic.

"Your father is back making a fool of himself in the field!"

"What do you mean, mother?"

"He volunteered to help his old friend do an excavation over at Avebury stone circle. They have been digging up a section of the Avenue together with some University students."

"That's good of him to give up his time to assist them. What's wrong with that?"

"He made an offhand remark to a visitor who turned out to be a journalist. He was speculating that some of the larger stones must have been levitated into place while the pits were dug with metal tools. She went and quoted him on that in a local rag. Now the other Archaeologists are wanting him to retract his comments. But you know how stubborn he is. I don't suppose you could go over to Wiltshire and calm it all down. You know how embarrassing I find it all when he goes off on one. You must have some leave coming up soon?"

"I've been planning on a shopping trip to Paris and was going to take in a show or two if I could get some cheap last-minute tickets. But I could do with a change of scene I must admit. I have been working too hard. If I can get some Eurostar tickets, I'll call him up and surprise him."

"Thank you, sweety!"

The call continued for a little longer with the two making small talk before Diana made her excuses and finished the call.

Diana felt strangely rejuvenated despite the unusual circumstances of her return to her room. She decided it was time to get up and get ready for work.

She slipped off yesterday's T-shirt, unbuttoned her jeans, unzipping and pulling the tight-fitting Levi's down in determined fashion. No pause for breath.

The small bathroom let the morning light through its net curtains. Diana gripped her shampoo and stepped into the shower cubicle. The reassuring rush of fresh, cold water tingled as it enveloped her slim frame. All looking good. Diana patted herself dry. All feeling good. Perhaps it was a dress day?

Moving back into her bedroom, she picked a suitable black dress. Black with lace patterns, crisp cotton, hanging just above her knees.

"Perfect," she said as she slipped into her low heels. She was ready to face the new day.

X - Calais

At the Office everything seemed to be under control, so she took some time out to look for some Eurostar tickets. As luck would have it, there was a discounted weekend break that took in Calais before crossing the Channel Tunnel to London. The price was a steal. She called up her dad to say she was coming so that he could sort her out a place to stay.

It also gave her time to meet up with her old site assistant Jess, who was excavating a field just outside of Calais for evidence of 'The Field of the Cloth of Gold' peace conference between Henry VIII of England and Francis I of France. Back then Calais was held by the English, much to the annoyance of every French monarch of their age. Both of the playboy Kings were trying to outdo the other, and further cement their earlier alliance against their common enemy The Holy Roman Empire under Charles V of Spain.

Jess was a fan of that era, which just happened to coincide with the lifetime of Diane de Poitiers. As a lady in waiting to Francis I's queen, it was likely that Diane had attended. Though Diana thought that the jousting and macho posturing would not be much to her taste.

Diana called up Jess, and it was decided that Jess would collect her from the station to go to her dig site so they could catch up before Diana re-joined her train for England.

The rest of the working week involved a lot of labelling of pottery shards, broken tiles and other Roman finds such as lead curses which tended to be deposited at holy springs by wealthy Romans to cause ills upon their enemies. It was an early form of Twitter.

On Friday morning, Diana finished her packing and drove her car to the station car park to make her connection to Calais. As the weather was still quite warm, she travelled light and wore her baggy trousers. If she took anything too smart or formal, it just made her father look more like a scarecrow than usual.

The TGV ride was fast and efficient through the flat northern heartlands of France. Fields of sunflowers shot by the windows while she was still in the Pays de la Loire region before reaching the green areas and industrial towns of the Pas de Calais.

At Calais station, she got off of the train, left by the main entrance and looked out for Jess.

Jess was around 30 with blonde hair and piercing blue eyes. She waved to Diana when she saw her. Jess ran over and hugged her like a long-lost friend. Their time as colleagues hadn't always been so jovial, but it was good to see those times had been largely forgotten.

"Hi, Jess. Lovely to see you again. I love your top. It's very shiny."

"Thanks. I thought I'd treat myself to a bit of gold since I'm digging the site of the ultimate bling – tents with cloth literally spun from strands of gold. I'm trying to get into their mindset."

"Hmm. Nice idea. So, where's your limousine?"

"Good old Diana. I'm afraid my tenure doesn't quite stretch to a new car. I have my trusty 2CV over here."

The two of them arrived at a somewhat beaten up old Citroen

2CV workhorse from the 1970s. Judging by its faded blue paintwork and giant daisies flower power was still at its height when the car had been new.

Jess unlocked the door for Diana, then lifted the door open.

"You best get in while I hold the door up. The hinge has rusted off, so it doesn't swing open. I don't often give lifts, so it's not been too much of a problem."

Diana got in, Jess closed the door and climbed in through the driver's door. They both burst out laughing once they were both sat down.

"Is that part of the mindset too?"

"No, Diana. They didn't have cars back in those days."

"True."

"So where are we going now?"

"I'll show you the site of a tiltyard we've recently excavated. It appears to be right on the border between the two camps. One side in English Calais, and the other side in France. If we're right, it's quite a find as it fits in with the recorded history of the time."

"That's great Jess. Is that where Henry VIII faced off Francis I in their jousts?"

"No. Protocol wouldn't allow monarchs to directly joust each other. They had to face each other's Champions. Etiquette had to be observed."

"Oh, I see. Medieval and Renaissance isn't my era. Though I have to learn up on Diane de Poitiers since she seems to have left traces in her garden at Chenonceau."

"Yes, she was quite a figure. We're not sure how much of the French court travelled here. Likely a fair bit, but a lot of the site has been ploughed out over time. The tiltyard was found under a thicket of hedge and a small hay store. We're lucky to have found any of it."

After a short while, Jess turned off of the main road and bumped along a country lane towards a cluster of portacabins and some parked minibuses from a local University.

"Welcome to my humble site, Dr Garry. I'm afraid it's no Château, but in its day this would have been spectacular. We'd dearly love to find evidence of the fountains that flowed with wine, but so far no luck."

"Thanks, Dr Felton. I look forward to seeing what you've found."

The two wandered past the parked vehicles and into the edge of the field where a large marquee had been erected over part of the dig site.

As Diana gazed up at it, the scene began to change.

A large bright gold tent looms ahead with gaudy flags, horsemen, jesters and noblemen everywhere. Behind me, as I turn are a more unadorned and more austere canvas structure where the ladies of the French Court can be seen. The ladies sleep in a dormitory tent with the nursery adjacent. We all sleep in 'cots' like narrow regular beds about eight or ten of us to a chamber with four or five beds per side like camp beds.

Up ahead I cross to the feasting/tournament tent across the courtyard. The wine fountain is in place, but it is not working due to a technical issue with the water/wine pressure. The King is not happy about it, but his most excellent engineers are looking at the problem. There are grandstands adjacent to the tiltyard – an English Grandstand and compound opposite – the French to the south, English to the north.

Inside the tiltyard, King Henry sits with Thomas More the keeper of the king's signet ring at this stage to his right (dressed in dark colours), Thomas Cromwell the Lord Chancellor is in red to his left. The Champions joust. At the Grand Finale, it is Henry VIII of England versus Francis I of France. This is entirely against etiquette, but neither absolute monarch cares about that. This is a sport. Henry is in white with the Cross of St. George surrounded by Tudor Roses in each of the four corners. He wears silver armour with gold gilding and decorations. Francis is in blue with gold Fleur de Lys, with the same concept of shiny armour with gold trim.

Francis is on a brown horse, Henry is on a black horse, Francis starts charging east to west, Henry gallops west to east. The first two runs they barely connect so are draws. On the third run, Francis is again running east to west, Henry is running west to east, Francis strikes under Henry's shoulder blade with his lance, toppling Henry to the ground. Francis turns and rides back, dismounts then crosses to help Henry to his feet. Henry is fuming, but shakes Francis' hand and pats him across the shoulder. Henry gestures to his squire, then his nobles and all head to the (southern) French banqueting tent where the winner hosts.

In the tent the English sit on one side (north), the French opposite (south), with a mixture on the connecting table to the east. The western side is open. Henry wears browns and burgundy colours with ermine trims, a squashed brown and burgundy hat/beret with a red feather. Francis is in a similar style but with blues and golds. Henry is flanked with Thomas Cromwell on his right and Cardinal Wolsey on his left. No women are present on his side. Francis (who likes his ladies) sits with his mistress. Queen Claude is unwell and has retired to her chamber with some ladies in waiting. I am staying with both of the Boleyn girls and Francoise plus a couple of other ladies in waiting. A handful of other nobles are present.

I have a small appetite and so eat very little. The food includes jellied pheasants and almond 'fancies'. I am wearing a cream dress with an embroidered bodice, plain skirt, matching cream and black bonnet with my hair tied into a basket. Mary Boleyn wears a blue dress with a white front to her bodice and her hat, red hair, pale skin, green/blue eyes. Anne Boleyn is in red-burgundy, with her blonde hair and blue eyes. Both do a dance in the square area between the tables, and especially in front of Henry. A jolly jig, twisting and turning. Mary is more exuberant. Henry watches intently, mesmerised by Mary. In the end, he stands up and claps, followed by the rest of the room. Cromwell and Wolsey move aside so that Mary could sit at Henry's right and Anne to his left. There are lots of giggling after this.

Later, Mary introduces Henry to me and the others. 'Enchanté' he says, his eyes light up at me and kisses my hand. My tummy feels apprehensive at meeting Henry, but I just smile politely.

Jess tapped Diana on the shoulder.

"You're quiet. Not like you. Are you OK?"

"I've just got a bit of an upset tummy. It's probably down to the journey or someone I've met. I mean something I ate."

Jess gave Diana a strange look before carrying on.

"Let me introduce you to Jacques, who is looking after our finds tray."

"Anything interesting today, Jacques?"

"Yes, actually today we have just uncovered some pheasant bones from what looks like a feasting area behind the tiltyard. It is fascinating to think how these nobles dined on such rich food then fought each other violently in jousting."

"Oh, interesting." Diana's tummy went tight as the sights she had recalled tallied with the evidence Jess' team had found.

"Does everything tally up with the recorded history, Jess?"

"Yes, so far. There was one day where the wind was too high so most nobles stayed in their tents and no jousting happened it seems. But every other day has at least a token entry in the history books."

"It's just a shame we're not 100% certain who was present on both sides. Henry's ambassador to the French court was Thomas Boleyn. So it's just possible that his daughters were here as they were serving as ladies in waiting to the French Queen. They originally worked for Henry's sister Mary but stayed on after she returned on the death of the old King. I think it's doubtful they would have met King Henry at that stage otherwise we would have heard about it and history may have been different."

"Yes, who knows indeed," Diana said it in a slightly incredulous manner.

Jess seemed a little puzzled by her friend's tone, frowning slightly before lightening up.

"I know what, take a look at this ring we found. Jacques – the best find tray if you please."

"Sure Madame. I go and get it."

The finds custodian returned with a small tray where a gold ring with a Fleur de Lys motif lay on a little cushion in the centre.

"May I pick it up, Jess?"

"Sure, go ahead."

The ring was quite sturdily built, quite masculine, with a dark blue gemstone or piece of glass inlaid in the centre. It was slightly familiar in some way. It was most likely a ring gifted by the French King to his nobles and Champions for their loyalty to him.

"Where did you find this, Jess?"

"One of the Uni diggers found it on what we believe was near the central point of the tiltyard. There's a certain residue of iron in places nearby. Possibly from weapons or even from the blood. Jousting was a dangerous sport, indeed. As you should know if you're learning about Diane de Poitiers. Her lover Henri

II was mortally wounded jousting in Paris some years after our tilt yard here. People died, people were maimed, and valuable trinkets were lost in the soil during the duelling. It may have been a noble sport, but it was also brutal."

Diana welled up inside at Jess's comments. She stayed quiet by marginally interested in Jess's site and finds.

They made small talk over a cup of coffee, and before too long, it was time for Jess to take her back to catch her train to England.

As Jess let out her colleague through her broken door at the station, she asked Diana to remember her to her father. He had once been her lecturer back in the days before he became too outspoken to be trusted with students.

XI - Avebury

The train journey to London was uneventful, if somewhat slow on the unimproved sections of rail on the UK side. She was able to catch up on her reading, plus take a peek at the local paper which had broken the story from her father. Diana tutted to herself a few times as she read the quotes. She loved him dearly, but sometimes he was a silly old duffer. No wonder her mother was horrified.

The tube journey from St. Pancras to Paddington was delayed by signalling issues. So good to be back in good old England!

Eventually, she got her train to Swindon and was able to enjoy the newly electrified line as it sped through Berkshire and on into the greens of Wiltshire.

Diana giggled as she saw a 'Famous 5' advert in the GWR magazine. Enid Blyton was synonymous with Corfe where she had grown up with her parents in a tiny cottage near to the Castle. Her father was good fun back in those days. She was always his favourite, she could tell. She took after him in many ways while her two sisters were more like their mother. At least Diana retained her mother's common sense, which her father lacked. He likely has Asperger's syndrome but had never been diagnosed. He indeed showed many of the signs.

After exiting the station, Diana looked around for the bus to take her down to Avebury. It wasn't a frequent service so she hoped she wouldn't have too long to wait. She also wished that she had enough British coins to pay the fare as they certainly wouldn't take the Euros she kept in the main section of her purse.

Sure enough, she found it and luckily had more than enough to cover a return fare coming back later in the weekend.

The bus bumped along the twisty roads up towards Avebury. It stopped several times at little stops at the end of country lanes by small hamlets, the Marlborough Downs on their left in the distance.

Eventually, it pulled in alongside what used to be an antique shop opposite the pub. It now appeared to be a smart crystal and jewellery shop. Very nice. Perhaps worth a visit before going back to France.

As it was still just about light, she knew her father would be at the dig site, so she wandered through the henge past the stones by the crossing point over the road, on past the trees and over the road junction into the field with the Avenue in it. This was a favourite place to visit after she had been shown the TV series 'Children of the Stones'. She could picture herself with the other kids exploring the stones and running down the Avenue into who knows what adventure! Today, she was a grown-up woman visiting her eccentric father on his dig site beside the Avenue as it wound its way towards West Kennet.

Eventually, she saw the place and could just make out her father's distinctive wide-brimmed hat peering down at a find he had just picked up.

"Hi, Pops. How are things?"

"Di. How lovely! This is a surprise."

"Not really, I did text you I was coming."

"Oh, yes! That's why I booked that extra room for the weekend. My mind's not what it was! Come over the cordon and sit on a chair."

"Thanks. So, what brought you here to take part in this dig anyway, Dad?"

"Well, it was funny, I was invited over by Brian who had just been given preliminary funding for a dig at Avebury. We had a coffee outside of the Pub here before wandering around the site. There are so many possible places to dig here that he was spoilt for choice. He also didn't want the 'Same Old' dig of the sarsens. So anyway, we got up and headed over the road into the field with the Solar stone circle behind the old chapel. We headed towards the Priest/ess 'Devil's' stone and the trees. Nothing was jumping out. So, I said to him 'let's go down the Avenue'. "

"He didn't seem very keen, but in the end, he acquiesced. It was after we reached the high point that I spotted all of the cattle grouped in a small area just to the side of the Avenue. I asked him 'What's there, Bri?'. He replied that there was a small geophysical anomaly and stone off of the Avenue there, but that nobody knew much about it. I suggested it was a vortex site as cows love that stuff. And where there's a vortex site, you tend to find temples or offerings in prehistoric eras. So, in the end, he agreed it was worth making the dig there. Or in fact, here."

"And does he or the others talk about vortices?"

"No."

"And why not, Dad?"

"Because they think the concept, and I, are a bit mad."

"Yes. I know. It's a bit full-on for most people. You raised me differently, of course. I was brought up with dowsers. But you know how uncomfortable the others can get. I'm cautious what I say in the press and in official circles. One to one, I have demonstrated the correlations between Earth Energy and archaeological features or anomalies. In private many of the youngsters 'get it'. But the old school and the gutter press just want to ridicule us if we open up about such things."

"But they need to know."

"In the fullness of time, they will do, I am sure. But don't go making a fool of yourself. That journalist you last spoke to is just out to sell her newspaper."

"But she seemed so nice and so interested."

"They always do Dad. They always do."

Doctor Garry senior frowned and shrugged his shoulders.

"Did your mother put you up to coming over to see me? I bet she's embarrassed by me again!"

"Firstly, I always like to come over and spend time with you. Our time together is so precious. But Mummy did speak to me and was worried about you. And of course, what others think. It's how she is. I had a free weekend that I'd have otherwise overspent shopping in Paris. So, the timing was good for me. I also dropped in on Jess while I was in Calais."

"You are a good daughter." He then whispered. "My favourite. Shhh."

"I know Dad, I know. I went into the family business, and the others didn't."

"Not just that. You've always had a spark that the others didn't. They got your mother's caution. You got my inquisitive nature. Now, look at you."

"I was just lucky, I guess. You brought me up well. Apart from when I fell down in your pit and broke my arm."

"You will never let me forget that will you?"

"No. Never. I was traumatised for a long time over that. It is a frightening experience for a child to be injured down in a deep dungeon and has to call out for help all night. If you hadn't found me the next day..."

"The visit by Social Services didn't help either I'm sure. They came after the search when we thought you'd run away."

"No. Nor Mummy's threat to divorce you if it happened to any of us ever again. The whole thing was traumatic for me. I had to have counselling years later. But it's good now. I'm over it. It's forgiven – but not forgotten."

"Well, I learned to keep a better eye on you after that. It made me a better parent. I think I had thought kids would bring themselves up if given enough freedom. I think that wide boundaries rather than no boundaries worked better in the end."

Diana gave her Dad a big hug.

"What was that for, Di?"

"You are a big old softy. But you do let your mouth run away from you sometimes!"

"Hmm. Was that for the bit about levitation?"

"Yes. I know that you've been chatting to the local dowsers here about the Moon phases changing the weight of the stones by a few kilos plus or minus. But there's a huge leap of faith between that and levitation. Merlin may have floated Stonehenge into place using magic according to the legend – but we archaeologists require proof. You know what we're like. And until that time, it's not the accepted version of history to suggest levitation to our colleagues or to the press. Or so Mummy gets to hear about it. It's sad but true, so please don't go getting overexcited and speculating to the Press."

"I know you are right. But it is a shame that our colleagues are closed off to non-physical theories."

"The Harry Potter generation of Millennials are more open to the concept of magic. Things will change. But for now…"

"I was born just a bit ahead of my time."

"If you stick around long enough, you may see those changes coming into the mainstream."

"I suppose so. The Time Team TV archaeologists were shunned by us as wreckers and amateurs. But they opened up the field to new talent and new ideas such as geophysics and using mechanical diggers. They did good field reports on sites that would not otherwise have been dug. Our attitudes changed completely. So I have seen it happen."

"If you like I can do a piece for the papers here about how you inspired me to take up Archaeology and how your jokes about left-field ideas helped me to give my digs a fresh perspective."

"That's a good idea. I have the lady's number. You can call her up and see if she'll come over. Brian's happy if you want to assist with our dig while you are here."

"A busman's holiday. Smashing. Though I've not actually dug here before. Which is odd as Bath's so close. Have you had any interesting finds so far?"

"Nothing earth-shattering, but various charms from the Roman era, plus much earlier goddess figurines. I'll show you them once the finds keeper is around in the morning."

"Yes, please, I would like that. Shall we head back to the pub and get a drink as well as a bite to eat?"

"Yes, why not indeed. The pub does a great pie and mash."

"I do miss pies. But the great coffee, French cuisine and croissants make up for it!"

"What's wrong with our coffee?"

"Don't get me started!"

The pair wandered back along the Avenue to the road junction, over the road and back to the Pub, crossing over the road again by the side of the bus stop and the newer crystal shop. The Pub was full of young Archaeologists with their pints amongst older locals who were either farmers or new age. There were one or two tourists, as well. Despite their different origins, ages and viewpoints, the atmosphere was jolly.

"What would you like Di?" Diana's father quizzed his daughter.

"Thanks, I will have a fruit cider, please. I used to like those when I was in the UK."

"OK. I'll see what kinds they have."

"Thanks."

They had sat in a quiet corner not far from the bar. While her father was waiting to be served a man in his forties came over and proceeded to engage Diana in conversation. It wasn't an uncommon occurrence for her – it just made a change for it to be in English.

"Hello, there, lovely lady. I've not seen you here before. Is that your boyfriend over there getting you a drink?"

"Uh, hello. No, he's my father. We just thought we'd come here for a quiet drink while I'm visiting."

"I can't believe that a pretty one like you is not with her boyfriend on a Friday evening?"

"No, he's in France while I visit my dad. He's had to stay behind to compete in the Karate competition. He got through to the finals and will be coming over here afterwards. I can introduce him if you like?"

"No, no, it's alright. I was just checking you were in safe hands. I'll leave you to enjoy your drink with your father. Good evening to you."

The man hurried away. Diana chuckled to herself. That line always seemed to work as a brush-off. Though one day somebody might call her bluff.

Diana's father returned from the bar carrying two drinks.

"Are you making new friends?"

"No, he just said hello, and I gave him my brush-off. He's not really my type."

"No. A bit too normal for you, I expect. I've ordered you chicken and mushroom pie with peas and salad but no chips. Hopefully, that will be OK?"

"Yes, thanks. I find chips too heavy. But I don't always have weird boyfriends, you know."

"What about Gavin?"

"OK. Gavin was a bit weird. In the end, it was either his love of Live-Action Role-Play or me. LARP won. He's probably running around dressed as a dwarf in pursuit of an elf as we speak."

"I don't doubt it. Before I forget, here's that journalist's phone number on her business card. I'm sure you can call her up in the morning."

"Yes. That was my plan."

Father and daughter spent the next hour or so discussing Diana's various ultimately hopeless boyfriends and her mother's reactions to them as well as to any other person or situation that wasn't exactly to her liking.

The chicken and mushroom pie was juicy and appetising. Her father's chips did look good, so she did help herself to them a few times before the meal was over.

After the meal was eaten and the drink was drunk, Diana was starting to feel somewhat tired. The early start and extra hour from the time difference had caught up on her.

“I think I need to turn in now Dad. Can we go back to your digs please?”

“Sure. The digs are quite good this time. I’ve got a bed and breakfast place just down the road in the village. It’s not very far. I think you’ll like it. The owner, Dee, is a nice lady. She makes sure I’ve got enough breakfast and cups of tea each morning. It is most pleasant. I’m not sure how Brian managed to get the funding agreed to cover it. But I’m not complaining.”

“That sounds great. I’ve only got my weekend bag. I have my jeans and t-shirt for excavation work, which is just as well. You lead the way.”

They left the pub and wandered down the road past the village shop, the Henge Shop and the entrances to both the National Trust barn area and the parish church. Eventually, they were outside a charming little cottage with what looked like her dad’s beaten up old Peugeot 205 outside.

“Harriot’s still going then? She must be a classic car by now, possibly a vintage.”

“Yes, she’s been a good old car. Nearly 600,000 on the clock. A good engine, but I’ve had a few spares put into her over the years. Tom’s still my mechanic of choice.”

“Amazing really. You’ve had the same car most of my life, and yet Mummy seems to change hers regularly.”

“Yes, she likes having a car to match her current mood. The estate cars were practical for you girls when you were kids at home. But now she’s got a 4x4. She never goes off-road on it, but all her friends have one, so that’s what she has.”

As Doctor Garry senior was fumbling with his key at the lock, an elegant lady in her early 60’s opened the door.

"Hello, Doctor Garry. This young lady must be your charming daughter Diane."

"Diana, actually. But yes, that's me. I'm pleased to meet you. Dee is it?"

"Yes, indeed. That's funny, I could have sworn the cards said I would meet a Diane today. And I must have misheard your father this morning. I'll have to use a different pack next time I give myself a reading."

"I'm sorry. A reading?"

"Tarot. I'm a Tarot reader as well as a bed and breakfast host. I'm usually pretty accurate. But we all have off days I suppose."

"Well, it's pretty close. And on my dig, I seem to hear the name Diane come up all the time. So, I expect your cards were picking up on that."

"Lovely to meet you, Diana. Let me show you up to your room."

The upstairs room was cosy. It was basic with an old flowery bedspread on top of a divan bed made up with sheets and blankets. There was a small sink in the corner.

As she was by now drained, she thanked Dee and called out "Goodnight, Dad" for her father to hear before she got herself ready for bed and snuggled down to sleep.

It was a tranquil street, and she was able to get a full night's sleep without being disturbed.

Around 7:00 am, there was a knock on the door.

"Hello, who is it?" Diana called out.

"It's Dee. Your father asked me to wake you up and ask you what you want for breakfast lovely."

"Oh, thank you, Dee. I'll just have a boiled egg, a slice of brown toast and espresso, please."

There was a slight pause before Dee asked. "Is that a strong black coffee, dear?"

"Uh, yes, that's correct. Thank you. I'll be down in a few minutes."

Diana changed into her jeans and t-shirt dig outfit to go outside of her room to have a lightning-fast shower in the small bathroom opposite her bedroom.

A few short minutes later, she was sat opposite her father at a small table in the cottage's dining room.

"Morning, Dad. This is a nice quiet cottage. I slept like a log. What's the plan for today?"

"We're extending the pit to go nearer the boundary fence away from the road. I'll let you strip off the layers most likely to be Roman, and you can see if we find anything interesting. That should keep us busy until lunchtime. I'm so glad that you like the room."

"OK. Sandwiches or pub lunch?"

"Neither. The National Trust has a small restaurant, and we shall go there. As a creature of habit, my friend from the Press tends to go there on a Saturday around 1:00 pm. We can perhaps catch her and put this blasted mess right, so your mother is back speaking to me. I'm sure she will like you."

"Yes, that sounds like a great idea."

Father and daughter politely ate their breakfasts and drank their drinks without speaking much more. Dr Garry senior finished his muesli and English Breakfast Tea slightly before Diana drank the last of her coffee.

"Shall we head over my sweet?"

"Yes, sure. I'm already as I know you like to go off straight after breakfast."

Ten minutes later they were at the dig site.

Diana was introduced to all ten of the archaeologists present on site. Most were students from local universities – including one from her own, Bath Sulis.

Pleasantries over, she was given a small patch to work on where the grass turf had been peeled back to reveal the layer just above the suspected Roman layer.

Picking up her trusty trowel, she proceeded to follow the standard protocol of scraping and recording. Though in truth, there wasn't much to record as it was a very uninteresting area she had been given it seemed.

It was very soon 12:45 and time to head over for lunch over at the National Trust restaurant for their possible press interview if the lady was indeed there.

As luck would have it, she was indeed there. It would seem that she was on her own on this particular afternoon so Diana's father approached her to ask if they could join her. She agreed and so Diana sat opposite the press Bloodhound. Only she wasn't so much a bloodhound as a petite redhead in her early 40's. Diana's dad had left them to get acquainted while he fetched some quiches and drinks for them both.

"Hello, I'm Dr Diana Garry. You have already met my Dad."

"Yes, he's a nice chap, but a bit eccentric. I just love the quotes he's given me over the last few weeks. Is he for real?"

"Well, he does tend to get a bit carried away. He started a black leopard scare a few years ago over in Dorset when one of his farmer friends joked about finding a dead calf on his land. Dad took it the wrong way and blurted it to the press. It turned out to be a tourist's dog from a nearby campsite. But it boosted the tourist trade for a short time, so the locals were happy."

"Oh, I see. That was a bit random."

"Yes, that's my dad. He should prefix most of his speculations with 'I've heard it said that…'. He doesn't really think that aliens levitated the stones into place. Like me, he knows that the evidence points to the use of waterways, dug-out barges and irrigation channels that have long since been ploughed out of the landscape. I can send you some maps and give you some quotes to go along with them that would make an excellent little article. I'll get dad to add something too."

"That would be great, here's my card with my e-mail and contact details on it."

"Lovely here's mine too."

"Thank you. Gosh, it's later than I thought. Lovely to meet you, I must dash."

And with that, the local paparazzi representative was gone.

Diana's dad arrived back in time to see his press friend disappear around the corner.

"Oh, that was a bit odd. Did somebody get upset?"

"No, but I promised her a good article, so she's probably going elsewhere to get another."

"Well, never mind. The quiche looks smashing, and I got us both a hot chocolate each."

"I don't do dairy, dad."

"That's OK as I got oat milk hot chocolates and vegan quiche. No dairy."

"Thanks, Dad"

Lunch was a pleasant catch-up with her dad. The afternoon was dull and uneventful. Back at the cottage, she sent out the information for the article. By the next lunchtime, the new story had bumped the old one off of its place of prominence, and Diana's mother was back speaking with her father.

So, mission accomplished, and after a pleasant break in Wiltshire, Diana was soon travelling back to France and her own dig. What more surprises were in store for her, she wondered.

XII - Morning

At her office, Diana read through her communications. She was particularly drawn to an e-mail thread between Jean Le Clerc and Jean-Pierre Du Lac his opposite number at the château of Anet, on the Seine to the east of Paris.

Jean had mentioned Diana's find and had suggested that she visit Anet, taking the bracelet with her. J-P had replied that he would love to see it, and could she come Thursday, in two days. Jean had, in turn, replied that he would need to check with Diana since she was busy as site manager and possibly unwell. At this point, Diana was typing a reply to say that she was perfectly fine and was keen to come along. She also added a question as to whether any Roman finds had been found in the grounds of Anet. Diana didn't know why she had added that, but she just felt it was the right thing to ask. She clicked send.

As Diana lent back from her screen and gently rubbed her eyes, eyebrows and lush eyelashes, she heard a knock at the door. It was Stan.

"Entrée," she called.

"Diana. You are in early today. Are you OK?"

"I'm fine. A bit of 'flu from overworking, I think. Did I pass out the other day?"

"Yes, I'm afraid you did. I helped carry you over to your room. Madame Albert tucked you into bed. It was lucky you didn't bump your head. What do you remember?"

"Not a lot. I was..." Diana's voice trailed away as she remembered the speaking picture and her dreams.

"I was just a bit giddy. It's the musty air in old houses – you know."

"I guess. Here, have your shot. It'll wake you up."

"Thanks. Nothing like a strong coffee to bring you around!"

Diana sat back and sipped on her double espresso.

"Anet. That rings a bell."

Diana lent forward and googled. 'Anet, château'. The Wikipedia page was the top entry. She clicked on it with her mouse.

"I knew it. The huntress statue. I was very taken with it at the Louvre. I had no idea it came originally from Anet."

"What's up?" Stan had peered over while his boss was muttering to herself.

"I just can't seem to escape Diana."

The two of them burst into fits of laughter as she and he realised what she had said. A couple of minutes later, she dabbed her eyes with a napkin to remove the tears of laughter.

"You know what I mean. Not me. The goddess. Artemis in all her forms. She crops up everywhere."

"Only since we found the bracelet." Replied Stan.

"True enough. But I've a strange hunch we'll find another Roman temple at Anet. I'm just awaiting a reply from..."

Her words trailed off as the new mail flag popped up on her screen. It was a reply from M. Du Lac.

"Well, I never!"

"Don't tell me. Roman temple remains at Anet?"

"Yes. When M. Du Lac was supervising the excavation of one of the demolition pits at Anet a few months back, they discovered some Roman tiles underneath."

"Silver glazed?"

"You bet! A probable Lunarium at another Temple of Diana. I may be jumping the gun, but it seems a likely outcome – if we can put in a test pit or two near those finds. I'll send a reply to M. Du Lac to make the request. I think I'll be doing some digging on my visit. Do you fancy coming on a house call Stan?"

"You're the Doctor. I think the gang can manage without us for a day or two."

M. Du Lac confirmed Diana's request and offered accommodation in the Château itself. Quite an honour for non-family members.

XIII - Anet

The drizzle didn't diminish the grandeur of the Château of Anet, yet Diana couldn't help feeling a little disappointed. In her imagination, Anet had seemed, well, bigger somehow. Now, as she approached the main entrance, a middle-aged man raised his hand in a friendly gesture before putting it down to shake the hands of departing guests.

"Au revoir Claire, Alex, Safe journey." The girl turned and smiled at Diana as she departed. She, like the château, seemed oddly familiar, yet unfamiliar at the same time.

"You must be Doctor Garry. And this must be your companion, Stanley?"

"Stanislav, actually," Stan replied before Diana could open her mouth.

"Aah, apologies Monsieur."

"No worries, just call me Stan."

Diana broke the macho posturing by offering her hand.

"Call me, Diana. Stan's my assistant. Please to meet you, Monsieur Du Lac, I presume?"

"Enchantee Mademoiselle. Beauty as well as brains I see!"

Diana unconsciously sighed. Frenchmen never seemed to

change; she thought to herself.

“Thank you. It was very kind of you to see us and let us stay. I’m looking forward to my time here.”

“Come in, come in. My home is your home.”

A ring of truth rang through Diana’s mind. Oh no, not again!

The Archaeologists stepped through the door of the entrance lobby. The hall was spacious, sparse, but elegant. To Diana’s mind, it looked not quite right. It was an odd feeling. A bit like visiting your home town years after leaving. The streets have the same names, yet the stores all look different. M. Du Lac noticed Diana’s slight frown and turned to speak to her.

“Anet was constructed from its foundations. An unenlightened owner saw it as a source of materials to sell – nothing more, nothing less. He was chased off by the villagers when they could accept no more destruction. What you see is short of two whole wings of the château that were demolished and sold off. Forgive me, but I know that as you have come from Chenonceau, there is something you must see first.”

Jean Du Lac excitedly hurried his guests to a separate building to the side that looked quite newly restored.

“This is the chapel. And here…”

M. Du Lac gestured to a magnificent black mausoleum topped with a beautiful statue.

“…Is the final resting place of Diane de Poitiers. She had Anet re-built to its finest state of magnificence and now – again – rests within its walls. Impressive n’est pas?”

Stan placed his hand on the lid of the mausoleum, tenderly feeling the smooth lines.

“Magnificent! The finest black marble unless I’m mistaken?”

"To be sure. It reflects the wealth and status of its owner and inhabitant."

Diana similarly reached over to admire the finish of the structure. But when she did a cold chill shot right through her, causing her to shiver. Yet it was a pleasant day, and the chapel was not at all chilly. It felt like somebody had just walked over her grave. But when Diana turned to look at her colleague he had gone. In fact, nothing was as she had just seen it at all, and neither was she.

I am eating food with Louis in the great hall at the medieval château of Anet. It is very dark and a bit tired in its decor – he at the head of the large oak table and I am on his left – our two daughters Francoise, age five and Louise age three beside me. Louis is eating beef off of his knife. I am not keen on this and give him disapproving looks in his direction. He cuts the meat and feeds himself off of his knife tip. He has a good appetite. I have a much poorer appetite. I am wearing an oatmeal utility dress for my everyday parental duties. Louis is thick-set with a square head. He has dark features, grey hair and some dark hair too. He is not a handsome man!

As Diana day-dreamed a picture of beauty and the beast came into her mind.

XIV - Ghosts

"Diana, Diana. Diana!"

Dr Garry awoke to see Stan standing over her. She was back in the chapel but was now looking out of the window.

"Sorry, I must have drifted off."

"No worries. Perhaps you should rest after your journey a while."

M. Du Lac took Diana's hand and led her back to the entrance.

"Here, Mademoiselle, er, Diana, let me take your bags from your car and show you to your room."

"Thank you, M. Du Lac."

"Jean-Louis, please."

"Here is my key. My bags are in the boot – the trunk. May I sit for a moment?"

"But of course. Sit on the bench here and take in the surroundings. The fresh air blown up from the Seine will soon wake you up, and if not, you can rest a while. The room you are staying in was said to be Diane's favourite. It seemed appropriate, somehow."

"That is extraordinarily kind of you."

"And for you, Monsieur, the adjoining room, said to be a favourite of King Henri II while taking in a hunt and enjoying the, shall we say, 'hospitalité' of Madame."

M. Du Lac chuckled as he carefully pronounced 'hospitalité'. He, of course, was eluding to the liaisons that would have taken place four and a half centuries earlier when Diane de Poitiers would have entertained her royal lover in the home that was bequeathed to her by her late husband – a man so much older than herself. But the home they had shared was a draughty medieval castle, not the Renaissance masterpiece that she had built for her and her young lover. However, that masterpiece had been sold brick-by-brick by a subsequent owner of the château. The current buildings had been rebuilt mainly by a more recent owner, lovingly restoring one block of the house and the chapel where Diane de Poitiers' remains now resided.

In Diana's flashback, the house had been completely intact in its mid-16th Century layout, complete with original tiles, statues and tapestries. It was a masterpiece of the French Renaissance, although the term 'Renaissance' was unknown at the time.

Now Diana settled down in the room that M. Du Lac had loaned her during her stay. It had been a bit of a strange day. What was happening to her?

As a student, she had laughed along with her peers as her lecturer poo-pooed the idea of reincarnation. And yet, could it be… Looking at Wikipedia and elsewhere there was some debate about Diane de Poitiers' birth date, yet one possibility stood out above all others: 31st December 1499. The last day of the 15th Century. The 31st December 1985 was Diana's own birth date. A maths graduate friend of Diana's was into 'numerology' and introduced it to Diana. From that, she could see that all the groups of digits were the same. 1499 adds up to 23. 1985 adds up to 23. 12 the same. 31 the same. And other dates matched the birth dates of relatives. It was all very intriguing and unsettling.Feeling suddenly exhausted Diana turned off her bedside lamp and laid her head down for sleep.

Just like in 'A Christmas Carol' the ghosts of the past visited Diana.

I feel content, if not happy. Our girls eat with us in the evening – soft-boiled veg and cut-up meat. Also, they eat some salad leaves in the summer.

In the bedchamber with its dark décor of mediaeval dark wood panelling that is a little scruffy, there is a four-poster bed – a bit dull – with dark burgundy surround darkened with age. I wear my cream nightgown. Louis wears a long beige nightshirt with a floppy hat. I kneel down to pray before getting into bed. Our lovemaking is something that I am repulsed by. I feel a sense of nausea and apprehension about it every time. I just lay on my back and let it happen. It is not enjoyable as it will be later with Henri. Louis is heavy too.

I lighten my life by planning and looking forward to having dinner parties. I have a good reputation for hosting parties and ensuring my guests are satisfied. They are very mediaeval affairs at Anet. There is a Great Hall. I sit to the left of Louis on a slightly raised dais with our guests nearby but lower. Minstrels play in-between in the mediaeval style. There is a Jester 'Poiçon' who is a great favourite and is very cheeky.

I wear a cream gown with a green bonnet in the renaissance style or the pointed hat with lace hanging down from its peak in the medieval fashion at different times. My gown is edged with a green band at the bottom with golden yellow crescent moons pointing up looking like melon boats. Our young daughters are both dressed in silky blue dresses with pointed hats. They always stay for the first couple of dances then are put to bed by me before returning to the banquet.

Once the dancing starts, Louis and I mingle with the guests. The men wear suede jacket outfits mainly, and the ladies are in silky gowns. My father, my brother and my sickly, simple half-sister five years my junior Mathilde who has something seriously wrong with her and is not expected to marry are all present. This reminds me of happy times, but I am always sad about Mathilde, who dies young soon afterwards.

XV - Coincidences

The cock crowed three times as bright autumnal dawn broke over the Château of Anet. Diana awoke and looked around the room. Where was she, who was she?

She put her hand towards the bedside table. Yes, her mobile was there, and the electric light. This is the 21st Century. She was Diana. Dr Diana Garry, respected Archaeologist.

"Phew!"

"So this is the place where my forebear spent her wedding night, and latterly entertained the King. Wow."

Diana turned her light on and started to jot down notes in her diary.

"No one will believe me, but with this much detail, it'd be foolish not to check out some of the facts."

At the end of her scribbling, there was a knock on the door.

"Come."

The door opened, and Stan stood in the doorway. The blue morning light, together with the bedside lamp lit the young man's features. His short stubble and outline looked…familiar.

"Mon Coeur."

"Sorry?"

"Oh, Stan, sorry. I mistook you for, um, someone."

"Yes – OK," Stan answered in a very unconvinced manner.

Diana was staring at her colleague in a somewhat off-putting way.

"Henri!" she whispered quietly under her breath.

"What's your star sign, Stan?"

"Aries. My birthday's 31st March. Don't you remember my birthday drinks? You know. The night Tom broke his leg."

"Oh. That evening. How could I forget?" She sighed.

"What year were you born, again?"

"'95, why?"

"Oh, just a sudden interest in numerology."

In her mind, Diana remembered that Henri II's birthday was 31st March 1419. Stan's was 31st March 1995. In numerology, you ignore the 9's. So the same digits recurred. She sighed to herself.

"What do you mean?"

"Just some coincidences with dates as well as other odd happenings recently."

"Your painting? How is that linked to my birthday? Are you sure you didn't bump your head too?"

"No. The Hindus and Buddhists strongly believe in reincarnation, while we in the west are taught to believe otherwise. What if they are right and we're wrong?"

"They also believe in sacred cows and multi-armed gods. Don't mistake low blood sugar for proof of the afterlife. You've been overworking recently. And perhaps you've got too close with this Diana/Diane business due to your name. Step back and stay objective."

"Yes. I guess." Diana sounded unconvinced now.

"I'll make myself decent and meet you for breakfast with M. Du Lac." She gestured for Stan to leave.

"OK. I'll see you, in…twenty?" Asked Stan.

"Yep. Sounds good to me." She replied.

XVI - The Charm

"Good morning, Diana! How did you sleep?"

An over-exuberant M. Du Lac greeted Diana as she arrived down to the grand dining hall off of the main entrance at the bottom of the stairs.

"Oh, fine thank you, Jean-Louis. It is an inspiring experience staying here. It was very kind of you to let us stay in the château."

"It was the least we could do. Your room is our 'honeymoon suite'. It is quite popular and was used only last night for newlyweds. It is said that Diane de Poitiers spent her wedding night in that room, or rather the room on that site, as it has been rebuilt twice since then, and once by Diane and once after the destruction. Some say she and her lover Henri's ecstatic screams can be heard on many a still night."

"Ah. Well, I must have slept soundly through that, but it was certainly, uh, memorable."

Diana and darted a look to Stan, and back to M. Du Lac.

"I believe that you have been looking after Diane's charm. May I see it please?"

"I guessed you might ask, so I did bring it down to breakfast with me. If it were Diane's charm, it would not be a stranger to these walls, I'm sure."

"No, indeed. Magnifique! Tres Bien. There can surely be no doubt!"

M. Du Lac carefully handled the delicate charm bracelet that had been neatly packed in cotton wool by the preserver. The original material had been separated from the jewels and the charm, so a replica black hemp band now supported the objects. After cleaning the gemstones looked like new, while the crescent moon was tarnished, but not severely corroded. Certainly not in a bad state for 450 years old, give or take. The original band dated to that era now that carbon dating had been confirmed.

"The old story from the local gypsies may be true after all. And the stones are royal moldavite you say. That is amazing. The Czech ambassador has visited Anet. I wonder if he knew of this connection?"

"Anything is possible. But the recorded history is decidedly thin. Although I have a hunch that the stones were a gift via Poland."

"Really? That is strange, indeed."

"Yes. The circumstances seem odd to me too."

"She was a fortunate lady to have such jewels and such a charm. Both the stone linked to the fountain of youth (the philosopher's stone), the charm from the local gypsies AND the ingestion of gold elixir. Her beauty and youth, even in old age, were legendary. Perhaps at least one of these things kept her so."

"I still don't quite get the connection to the Diana Temples and the cult of Diana. A staunch catholic defender of the faith, feted by the Pope, how did that fit together?"

"I can help explain!" M. Du Lac started.

"In the middle ages, there were conflicting factions in the mother church. Secret societies and sects abounded. In France, the Black Madonna, 'Our lady' and Mary Magdalen cults were potent. Diana, a symbol of the divine feminine principle, found fertile ground with the elite women. Diane de Poitiers' mentor was one such follower. It is said that all of them had stained glass windows in their lady chapels that reflected their beliefs. The Diana cult predated the specific Magdalen cult but was one, and the same movement absorbed into the church. It was natural that Diane should revive that aspect. The French catholic influence in Rome ensured it was not outlawed and even grudgingly encouraged."

"That's amazing. But is there documentary proof?"

"Not really, but even Jeanne D'Arc was linked. Diane was fascinated by her when she stayed by the tower in Rouen where Jeanne was imprisoned. It was a dangerous structure, so her husband warned her off. Even so, she continued. Strong women gravitate together. But I do have some old notes that may help."

"That sounds at odds with the history books. Are you sure about this?"

"Oh, yes. It may sound very 'Dan Brown', but every fantastic historic plot has a grain of truth in it. The gypsies, originating in Egypt potentially, also revered the goddess Isis and identified with Mary Magdalen, who some say was a priestess of Isis. They also respected Roman and Celtic sites. The ruined temple of Diana was possibly why they settled here."

"Really?"

"Yes. And the reason the castle was sited here was due to the fresh spring sacred to Diana before."

"The need for fresh water in castles under siege and the link between water and goddesses, and indeed birth are well known."

"Sacred geometry played a part too. We have had dowsers visit here. They also visited the Pont de l'Alma, where your Princess Diana sadly died. It is the site of another Diana/Artemis temple. Both on the Seine. And close to Diane de Poitiers' Paris residence. Almost as if she knew too."

"Whoa! You are going too fast for me now. I started with a Roman dig, and now we're getting contemporary. I'm an archaeologist, not a conspiracy theorist!"

"But of course. Apologies, Mademoiselle."

"My near-namesake could not have known about Roman temples in the Renaissance period. Surely they were long forgotten?"

"Generally, that is so. But," M. Du Lac sighed. "Certain secret schools seemed to know these things. The Templars, Cathars and Masonic groups appear to have had old knowledge passed down to them."

"Oh, come on, I'll leave that to Dan Brown!"

"No, no, the Notre Dame Cathedrals of 'Our Lady', certain later priories and Cathar strongholds were built on former pagan sites associated with goddesses such as Isis. From the pattern of her residences, it is either a fantastic set of coincidences or Mme. de Poitiers and possibly her Mentor Anne Beaujeu were also privy to some of that information!"

"I see your point. But I'll go with 'interesting coincidences' for now, thank you."

The rest of breakfast was a little subdued as Diana contemplated the possibilities while Stan and M. Du Lac discussed rugby and football games.

XVII - Temples

After breakfast, M. Du Lac led the way to the site of the lunarium remains in the château grounds.

"Fascinating," said Diana as she surveyed the pottery shards in a side ditch.

"The roof tiles are exactly the same as the ones we found at Chenonceau. I was expecting some variations, but as far as I can see, there are none. Obviously, the lab results can confirm that."

"Stan, did you pack the GR Rig?"

"Yes, I did. It's a big box to pack, but with the potential here and the short length of our visit it did make sense to have it."

"Precisely."

"M. Du Lac, with your permission, I would like Stan here to use ground radar around this area. It will also show up any foundations in the ground belonging to the château or outbuildings."

"Of course, Diana. But could we have copies of any printouts that you produce, for our museum display?"

"It shouldn't be a problem, um, John-Louis. I can clear it with Paris, I'm sure."

Stan wandered back to their car while Diana prodded a metal prong lightly through the turf around the ditch.

When Stan returned, she pointed to a low wall a few metres to the north of the lunarium site, then gestured along to the edge of the border.

"OK. I see the spread that you want. Leave it to me."

"Great. Let's see if the layout is the same too."

"John-Louis, may I see the spring, if you have uncovered it yet, please?"

"Of course. It is just behind you. Our gardener has been using it for a long time. He had thought it was a leaking pipe until he found the water mains further up the lawn."

"If I can just get an unspoilt sample of the water, I can send it for analysis against the Chenonceau sample."

"What do you expect to find?"

"Maybe nothing, maybe a link. Very deep alpine water surfaces all over Europe. Where it comes up in a pure form, we sometimes see a cult centre appearing in deep pre-Roman Times. The cult after became linked to a Roman goddess."

"The sacred water – feminine link. I always wondered about that one."

"The water of life. Birth and new life. Females give birth. It is logical, although I've often wondered about a deeper meaning."

"If there was, I doubt if we would discover it!"

"No, maybe not." Diana sighed and moved towards the ditch where the broken pottery was found.

"Could I dig a test pit here – no more than a square metre?"

"Of course. But please put it back afterwards. Claude is very proud of his lawns!"

"Thank you, Jean-Louis. I have some tarpaulin in the car, along with the rest of my equipment. I'll go and get it so I can make a start. I'll consult with Stan and yourself when we have a better idea of the site to dig."

"Can I get you a coffee while you were preparing, Mademoiselle?"

"That would be great. An Americano and perhaps similar for Stan, thanks!"

"My pleasure, Diana. Happy hunting."

"Funny. But no game here I fear."

The next half hour or so was spent getting the shovels, tarpaulin and measuring equipment out of her car before consulting with Stan over their coffees. The initial plot from the radar indicated a stone target wall near to the broken tiles, so Diana decided to dig the test pit there. M. Du Lac was happy as it was the barest part of the lawn.

Diana stripped the turf back while Stan started the spadework. At a level of approximately 20 cm he struck a solid piece of rock or wall tile, so levelling off the site at that level the rest of the excavation could proceed using the smaller trowels.

The pits yielded several pieces of tile from the lunarium, which were carefully recorded and placed in the finds tray. A small Roman brooch followed a little later before they bottomed out on the wall remains.

The temple walls had been substantially built using the highest quality faced limestone, decorated with red and black plaster. On what had obviously been the inside of the wall was a section of small mosaic tiles making up a section of tiled floor that stretched to the edge of the test pit. Diana called to Stan to ask him to bring a bucket of water and a sponge. Carefully and slowly, Diana wiped away the ingrained dirt and grime to reveal a stunning gold surround with a small deer.

As more of the pattern was revealed to her, she could soon discern the shape of an upturned crescent moon shining above the pale face of the beautiful goddess: Artemis, or Diana's namesake in its Greek form. This was a stunning find. It also would reinforce Dr Herbage's controversial view that the majority of sacred sites in France were dedicated to a goddess, rather than to a god.

Before the Christian church usurped idolatry, the sacred feminine was pre-eminent in both Roman and pre-Roman religion. It could also help to confirm the legends of 'swan boats' that brought virgin priestesses from the great temple of Artemis at Ephesus to the shores of France through the Greek colony of Marseilles. And indeed, the notion that Mary Magdalen said by some to be herself an Egyptian priestess of Isis was drawn to the shores of Gaul to seek the sanctuary of her sisterhood was tantalising. Diana's mind wandered back and forth through such notions as she sat on the edge of the test pit, kicking her legs and sipping her bottle of Evian. And as she daydreamed the scene before had changed.

I am inside the chapel in Anet, finely dressed in black velvet edged with exquisite lacework. My arms are draped in fine silk of black, my slender, long arms ending in long-fingered hands. On my left hand's ring finger sits a beautiful ring with an 'H' and a 'D' intertwined, surrounded by a ring of 12 small stones alternately sapphires and diamonds all set in gold on a band of gold. Although it is not visible, I know that the inscription reads 'Pour Diane, Mon Coeur, Mon Vivre' – for Diane, my heart, my life. I am kneeling before the altar, the pungent smell of the incense burning with the scent of Frankincense, lavender around it, in front of me a window showing Mary Magdalen with her bottle of ointment. I make the sign of the cross to the image.

"Diana?" The scene faded as Stan spoke to her. "Are you OK?"

"Uh, yes – fine. Thanks."

"OK. I have finished recording the test pit. Quite an important find. You must be very pleased. A major temple of Diana, previously unknown and the high-status mosaic in good condition. It will make a fine article in 'The Antiquarian' magazine at the very least. I wonder if I might suggest we ask Paris to sanction geophys?"

"Thank you. Just luck, and a little woman's intuition Stan. But it is not a bad idea bringing in geophys. If Jean-Louis agrees we may well get to dig here next year. I think the cost of maintaining Anet is quite high, so a new tourist attraction outside of that Diane De Poitiers' story might be attractive to him."

"I would think he would be thrilled."

"Let's back-fill the pit, place the turf back, then look for a place to eat. I think we should invite Jean-Louis along. He's been great so far, and I'm sure he'd come along. Maybe he'd even give us some more insights into Diane."

"Hmm. I think the old rascal would go out to dinner with you. I'm not so sure Jean-Louis wants me along. I can see how he looks at you. I'd watch him if I were you, else you could end up living here permanently!"

"Stan! I'm not interested in him. But it's nice to get some attention for once. When I'm on the dig, the younger girls in their vests and shorts get all of the attention from you guys. If you had X-ray eyes..."

"Diana! I'm always professional... And discreet." Stan winked.

"You guys are all the same. I personally like some attention but not oggling. Young Cynthia with her blonde hair and, uh, chest, seems to have her admirers."

"She's a bit too giggly and immature. I prefer the more mature type," replied Stan.

"Moving swiftly on..." Diana smiled. "I think I'll swing by Jean-Louis' office for restaurant ideas, then swing by my room to freshen up. I feel in the mood for my nice frock."

"Don't tell me - black and white - just like Diane de Poitiers' ? You'd almost think you were her."

"You'd not believe me if I told you. But yes, it is black and white. Jean-Louis will be eating out of my hand."

"You are intriguing me. Just don't get yourself burned."

"I'm a big girl. But first I'm going to pop back to Diane's tomb."

"Be careful, you passed out last time."

"I will be. I know what to expect now."

"Well, if you are sure."

"Thanks, Stan."

Diana wandered out from the main part of the château, over the drawbridge, along the road and into the funeral chapel. There, stately and magnificent in its white and black form was Diane's tomb.

This time Diana braced her feet against the black plinth at the front end opposite the altar and leant into the tomb, gripping the scalloped edges of the lid. Strange feelings of nausea rose up in her mind. Were these Diane's last feelings as she slipped away from toxic poisoning due to imbibing gold all her life to retain her youthful features? Perhaps.

Diana concentrated, using her knowledge of meditation to connect. She consciously sent feelings of love and nurturing to Diane, much as she gave herself when experiencing her own monthly stomach cramps. The feeling of nausea in her throat subsided and was replaced by an intense feeling of unconditional love in her heart. Was this a gift from Diane as a thank you?

After a few minutes, Diana moved away from the tomb, curtsied a 'Thank you' to Diane's funerary statue and left the chapel. She turned and looked back as she reached the door. At that moment a shaft of light picked up the tomb, then reached the door, lighting up her own face. Was that a to coincidence, or Diane returning her thanks? Diana walked back to the main entrance and unlocked the heavy door with the key Jean-Louis had loaned her.

XVIII - Dinner

That evening Diana washed in the simple sink beside the bed in the château's former guest range. She chose a simple gold chain with a small Egyptian 'Ankh'on it to place around her neck, then put in some simple amethyst earrings set in silver. Then, inexplicably, she picked up the bracelet that had been Diane's. The original leather band had been replaced by a replica while the original had gone to be preserved.

Diana tied the cords carefully around her wrist. It was a good fit. She decided to keep it on.

Applying a generous spray of lavender deodorant - her favourite fragrance - she was ready for her LBD. The little black dress. Was it Diane de Poitiers who paved the way for this elegant item? One which no girl's wardrobe would be complete without? Perhaps. The silky fabric brushed against her thighs as it slid over her waist, stopping above her knees as she wiggled it down.

Diana didn't possess too many heels due to her height (and profession), so she opted for a low-heeled court shoe in black patent leather.

She sat down at the dresser – a silver one that may have been Diane's. (Nobody was sure as her possessions from Anet were scattered by a subsequent owner and the revolution. This one was found in the village and bought by the château's current owners). Diana applied a small amount of black eyeliner below her eyes, but as usual, she did not use any other makeup, preferring the natural look.

She adjusted her clothing to show her modest cleavage to its best effect.

“Good girl. You’re looking hot but stylish,” she said to herself quietly.

Her phone rang. It was Stan.

“Hi, Diana. The institute rang me. They want a report from me on the dig status back at Chenonceau – just the groundwork – so nothing for you to worry about. But it does mean I’ll need to give tonight a rain check. Monsieur Du Lac will be pleased.”

“You’re having a laugh, Stan. I’d cancel, but I’m all ready. But if I find out this is a setup I’ll be having words with you.”

“Would I wind you up? I’m very hurt.”

“Yes, you would, and you’re not.”

They both laughed.

“Okay, catch you later, Diana. Have a nice time.”

“I will do. Speak in the morning, at breakfast.

Diana looked at her watch, realised it was time to go down, so she grabbed her black velvet bag and proceeded downstairs.

Jean-Louis Du Lac was wearing his suit, adorned with a minor ribbon of the ‘Legion D’Honneur’ from his time serving in Rwanda is a peacekeeper during the genocides there. He and his unit had safeguarded an entire village of women and children from an angry mob from the rival tribe. All without bloodshed. A photo of President Mitterrand presenting him his ribbon still hung in his office.

“Ooh la la, Diana, you look stunning tonight.”

"Thank you, Jean-Louis. You look dashing yourself. I hope that the restaurant deserves us!"

"Le Manoir D'Anet is a fine establishment. It is said that Claude's Great Grandfather prepared the feast for Voltaire's visit to Anet. It may be true. Where is your colleague, Stan?"

"He can't make it. Important business to attend to. He sends his apologies."

A big grin erupted and disappeared again nearly as quickly across Jean-Louis's face.

"Oh, that is a shame. The duck is perfect this season, and I know that Claude had prepared some Czech style pickled cabbage for Stan's delight." Jean-Louis feigned disappointment in Stan's absence.

"I'm sure we will manage."

Diana lifted her arm to allow Monsieur Du Lac to link his arm in hers.

They went out through the doors at the bottom of the grand staircase, crossed the gravel courtyard and exited the château through the main gate. Crossing the main road to the left of the war memorial, they walked along towards the restaurant. Jean-Louis was telling Diana his corny jokes in English.

At the restaurant, Claude hastily switched the tables to give Jean-Louis and Diana a more intimate setting. He lit a candle, poured them each a glass of kir and pushed Diana's chair into the table.

"Merci, Monsieur," she said.

Jean-Louis sat down. He peered at Diana in a slightly curious way.

"My, my. I don't quite know how to say this, but you do have more than a passing resemblance to Diane de Poitiers. It is incroyable. How can this be?"

Diana's face flushed. "She was a strawberry blonde of incomparable beauty. I'm just an ordinary dark-brown haired girl. It is surely a trick of the light." Although inside Diana's stomach tightened and the little voice in her head said: "He's right."

"Perhaps, Mademoiselle, but perhaps not. I can see you are passionate and driven like the mistress of Anet. Perhaps she has returned for some reason in the form of you."

"Reincarnation, although possible, in the case of some inexplicable cases of children who appear to know about a past existence in great detail, is still unproven."

"In one of Voltaire's lesser-known memoirs, he likened Madame Louise Du Pin to Diane de Poitiers. 'She simmers with the great beauty of the Huntress, silver, bright and incorruptible. Diana reborn once more as the mistress of Chenonceau.' And without Madame Du Pin Chenonceau would have been razed during the revolution. It was as if Diane had returned to save her beloved château. The heyday of that magnificent château was actually in the Enlightenment rather than the Renaissance. Just compare their characters to each other and perhaps to yourself."

Oh, please, Monsieur Du Lac. I'm a simple archaeologist, not a feminist icon. I never burned my bra. Besides, wouldn't Diane have wanted to save Anet? From what I've seen it fared quite severely in the Terreur, while most of Diane's belongings and even her remains were cast to the winds. Why save Chenonceau?"

"Simple, she truly loved Chenonceau. Whilst Anet, she rebuilt as a duty to her late husband. Given a choice, she would have chosen Chenonceau, and her mortal remains would be there; instead, Madame Du Pin lies there while Diane was as good as banished to Anet. If she loved Anet them, it was tinged with sadness and loss of Henri, loss of Louis De Brézé and loss of Chenonceau."

"Isn't it possible Diane came back here to bring Anet back to life. Perhaps in your family?"

"Ho, Ho, I think not my dear. We're simple farmers, not educated like yourself and those ladies. Do you have your own library at home?"

"Of course, I'm attached to a university. I have several hundred books on history and archaeology back in my childhood bedroom. My mother despairs of me."

"I think that as another clue, my dear. But I have taken up enough of your time. I can see Claude is arriving with the scallops. I hope you approve. He didn't want to interrupt us, so I signalled to him. And the duck will be OK for you?"

"Both fine choices Monsieur. But small portions as I must watch my figure."

"I'm sure there are many others who do that, my dear!"

"You are a rogue." Diana's face flushed once more.

"So what brings us here tonight, Diana?"

"Ahh. You're most perceptive Monsieur." Diana sliced off a section of her scallop, dipping it in the creamy white wine sauce, before putting a small part in her mouth. She chewed, swallowed, then smiled at monsieur Du Lac before making a considered reply.

"I'm hoping to approach the institute to ask them to fund a full-scale dig at Anet. The site is beyond the mosaic floor and is likely to uncover a major mosaic floor as well as the temple to Diana. A site like this could put Anet back on the map, putting money on the table for repairs to the château here. I can see that the battlements need repairing for a start. If you are agreeable, I'm sure I can put forward a strong case. What do you say?"

"Mademoiselle, you may yet be our salvation. I will speak to the family and suggest they agree." He smiled.

"Only last week I was struck by falling rocks from the battlements. Repairs could not come too soon."

Diana smiled and took another bite of her scallop.

"Excellent." She offered Monsieur Du Lac her hand to shake. But of course, he leant his head down and kissed it instead.

The rest of the meal proceeded smoothly. With a fair amount of small talk and a few corny jokes from Monsieur Du Lac.

At around 10:30 pm, Diana was starting to fade badly, yawning into her hands politely.

"Oh, my dear, you are tired. But we have finished our meals, I do not need to have my brandy tonight. Did you enjoy the duck and Claude's crème caramel?"

"Yes, indeed. But please, have you brandy, I'll last a bit longer. But after we should get the bill. I'll pick up the tab. My treat."

"No need. Claude takes ducks from the estate. So, we of the château entertain here often."

"You're too kind. Perhaps you will come over to view the dig at Chenonceau and take a bite with us there?"

"Perhaps indeed, it has been a long time since I met up with Jean Le Clerc. We have stayed in touch since the château summit a few years ago."

"Let's check our diaries and get you over before the dig season ends."

"Of course. But now I will walk you back to the château."

"Thank you."

Jean-Louis nodded to Claude, helped Diana up and put her coat around her shoulders.

The stroll back to the château was short and crisp. Diana and Jean-Louis exchanged a few more pleasantries. The soldier figure at the war memorial stood sentry over the road as they crossed back to the château. The strong, yet crumbling, walls appeared to glow in the moonlight as the custodian and archaeologist crossed the bridge over the now dry moat. Jean-Louis dropped his bunch of keys, exclaiming a few choice words as he bent down to pick them up again. Taking the correct key in his hand, he quickly unlocked the door and pulled it open.

"Après Vous, Mademoiselle."

"Merci beaucoup, Monsieur." Diana replied.

At the accommodation range, Jean-Louis paused and turned to Diana.

"Merci beaucoup, Mademoiselle. Diana, I had a lovely evening. You are a charming lady."

Why thank you, Jean-Louis. I enjoyed myself too. It is nice to let my head down once in a while."

"Would you consider a nightcap?"

"I don't think so, but I appreciate the offer, Jean-Louis."

"Ahh well, a bon nuit, sweet dreams Diana." Jean-Louis bowed down and kissed the archaeologist's hand.

Both parties smiled. At the top of the steps, Diana went to the right to her room as Jean-Louis went to the left. The clocks in the stateroom chimed 11:00 pm as Diana reached the door to her room.

Diana quickly changed for bed, remembering to hang her dress on the back of the door before she slipped under the covers. As she slept images of Anet in its grandeur flashed through her mind. The images changed as the château declined, the buildings fell into disrepair, the grounds became untended, and the buildings were demolished as Anet was nearly wiped off the map.

Images of Diane de Poitiers' funeral chapel being forced opened by the revolutionary guards to use the space for their meetings. Images flashed on as others opened the lid of the tomb, desecrating Diane's grave and disrespectfully moving her remains out of the coffin and out of the funerary chapel on a makeshift hemp sack stretcher, women using shears to cut at her beautiful golden locks of hair. Her remains thrown unceremoniously in a hastily dug a pit.

Diana woke with a start and a scream, the perspiration running down her skin. Tears rolled down her cheeks. But oddly, she found herself whispering "I forgive you."

The images in her mind faded, and she fell back into a deep, pleasant sleep.

XIX - Return

It was time to return to Chenonceau.

Jean-Louis had been very attentive at breakfast, bringing Diana fresh crepes, black coffee and fresh croissants. Diana got the impression he would be staying in touch. With the potential for whole new dig, it was worth keeping in his good books even if she wasn't in the mood for romance.

The car was duly packed, the finds tray and the bracelet packed neatly into the boot.

Jean-Louis shook Stan's hand before embracing Diana for a kiss on both checks. "Au Revoir, Diana."

Stan gave Diana an inquiring look, which made her wince.

Once on the road, Diana laughed and said: "No – he's not my type!"

Stan burst out laughing. "Jean-Louis's definitely an admirer – watch out!"

As the miles went by the now-familiar Loire Valley landscape was appearing. Vast fields of sunflowers sporadically littered the roads, the hazy sunshine lighting up the long stems and large flower heads still in bloom. As her mind wandered, Diana did have a strange hunch that Roman sites and her Renaissance

Duchess were somehow interlinked.

Rouen was another place where Diane de Poitiers had lived with her husband. It was at a castle in the town, itself the site of a Roman amphitheatre that Diane had spent a fair amount of her younger days. Perhaps a temple of Artemis had also been in existence there? But the castle was completely ruined, with only a reconstructed tower still in existence. It was a small needle in a big haystack. But just perhaps... A weekend away would do wonders!

A little way before arriving at Chenonceaux, Diana thought she would broach the subject with her colleague and friend.

"Stan. I have a little blue-sky thinking for you."

"OK. What's on your mind, Diana?"

"The Renaissance – Diana, Mediaeval – Joan of Arc, Black Madonna's, Templars - Our Lady Notre Dame cathedrals, Dark Ages – legends of Mary Magdalen, Roman-era – Artemis. Is there a common thread here or do I see patterns that don't exist here?"

"Hmm. There is a female thread glinting through what is thought of as a very male-dominated era, certainly. But witches were still being burned and Pagan beliefs outlawed, so it couldn't have been so widespread or blatant could it?"

"Perhaps in France, there were parallel paths – understood, but unwritten. A yin for their yang. The cult of Isis was prevalent within the Roman world. Vying with Mithras worship and Christianity. Emperor Constantine redefined Christianity to confirm Jesus' divinity and combined some Mithraic aspects. That is well known. But perhaps other strands persisted long after. Some churches and cults differed widely for a long time. Many heretics were burned and persecuted for their beliefs. Yet legends persist."

"Go on. You are in full flow. Carry on."

“Right. And remember I’m not Dan Brown. These legends were known long before. But let’s expand wildly. There’s both the truth and what people believe to be true. The two can be quite different. Let’s say that Mary Magdalen was a priestess of Isis. She married Jesus, an Essene, for whom Pagan marriage was possible. The betrothal brought together two houses - that of David and that of Solomon. They produced two or three children - one daughter and at least one son. Call them Jessica, Joseph and Jesus junior."

"Sometime after the last supper and crucifixion, it became dangerous for them all, so the family split up. Using trading links and Joseph of Arimathea's boat Mary Magdalen and her daughter plus younger son arrived at the Greek port of Marseilles and join up with other exiles and perhaps Isis followers in the south of France. The Greek Artemis, Egyptian Isis and Roman Diana together with other goddess cults appear to blur together in the later Roman-era.”

“Oh, wow! But, Stan, surely that’s just pure fantasy and conjecture isn’t it?”

“Why? I mean, perhaps so. But the facts and the legends often indicate otherwise. The cults of Artemis and Isis became Christianised under Mary Magdalen. Templars seem to have an allegiance to her more than to Jesus. They paid for the ‘Our lady’ - the Notre Dame cathedrals throughout France. Did they further base the design on the Temple in Jerusalem and use plundered gold to pay for them too?”

“Oh – Conspiracy alert Stan! You can’t seriously buy into any of that. We’re meant to be serious archaeologists, not Erich Von Daniken!”

“Much of it, perhaps. But what people in France believed may have been more than we can find palatable. If “Our Lady” was a nod to Mary Magdalen not Jesus’s Mother Mary then we have a thread from Roman Times until the Medieval and perhaps beyond. One that joins all of yours together."

Diana gulped. In many ways, this rang true. But it shouldn't. It was fringe history. She would be a laughing stock if she tried to present the links in archaeological circles.

"But Diane de Poitiers was a devout Catholic who encouraged the burning of Protestants as heretics."

"Protestants were heretics to her. But that doesn't mean she would have considered all things to be heresy."

"Go on."

"If goddess worship, disguised as Black Madonnas and the veneration of Mary Magdalen – "Our Lady" - was deeply ingrained in French Society or more correctly, in French royalty – that some claim descends from Jesus and Mary Magdalen. Perhaps Diane De Poitiers' cult of Diana was perfectly acceptable and little more than just a classical revival combined with chivalry."

"Fine. It sounds plausible. But without hard archaeology or historical documents, we're still way out there on the fringe."

"Yes. But you did ask for 'blue sky' thinking."

"And that's what I got. Thanks, Stan. I got what I asked for."

The last few minutes of the journey were spent in silence as Diana tried to absorb the speculations that Stan had brought to the fore.

One thing was certain. She'd be on the road to Rouen. And perhaps on the road to ruin too. But the search for truth was strong in her. The daughter of a maverick. A proud maverick.

XX - Rouen

Stan parked the car. He had taken over from Diana midway through as they often did on trips. It meant both could work on arrival without being too tired.

Diana assisted in bringing in the sample boxes and find trays from Anet. Some pieces would go straight on to Paris for assessment at HQ along with her report. Certainly, Anet had to be given a closer look.

The report over Anet was strangely straightforward for Diana to produce. It was fascinating to find the second lunarium within weeks of the first – especially given their rarity.

With the report done and the samples packed up after being photographed, they were boxed and sent to HQ along with the weekly site report via a courier.

With all the admin done, Diana realised it was lunchtime - her lunchtime being 2.00 PM. Time for a stiff coffee to set up for the afternoon.

'Lunch', as it was, over she felt relaxed enough to look at Rouen. Her money being a bit tight she looked at budget hotels on a booking website. At least it was off-peak, so prices were reasonable. Two nights on Friday and Saturday would be enough. The cathedral, château ruins and the market square would be her starting point.

The rest of the week was relatively uneventful. The excavation was digging out more of the temple, but with bones and charred remains needing to be sifted out of the soil, it was painfully slow, and no new significant finds were made. Each morning Diana submitted a report on the preceding day's dig.

Finally, it was Friday afternoon. She drafted her report ready to tweak and send on Monday upon her return.

Stan was off visiting his parents in Czechia for the weekend, so Diana was on her own. It was just a matter of returning to her room to retrieve the bag she had packed in previous evenings to put in the boot of her car. The only difference being that her car was in the garage, so she had a courtesy car. It was quite lovely - a Citroen DS3, red with a black roof. DS was short for 'déesse' - goddess, believe it or not, so DS3 was a triple goddess.

Diana chuckled as there was no escape from her work in this car. After getting used to the clutch and the gearbox, the car drove quite smoothly. She took the most direct autoroutes and route national roads to the city of Rouen.

Heading for the river, Diana was able to find her hotel quite easily and park nearby, feeding the parking meter with enough Euros to cover her stay. The hotel room had a balcony overlooking the cathedral. Beautiful.

Diana had allowed herself enough time to get ready for a quick wander around the city before it got dark. She freshened up, popped in a pair of tasteful pearl earrings, then slipped into a figure-hugging black and silver print dress, completed by a couple of low-heeled boots. She brushed her long brown hair and moisturised her to face with some aloe vera. No need for makeup.

She went down the few flights of stairs, exited through the main doors and made her way to the road running parallel to the river. When she could see the cathedral directly up the hill from her, she turned up toward the old town. She was tempted to go inside the great church, but in the event followed the main mediaeval shopping streets towards the church of Saint Joan of Arc.

As she was passing the small garden outside the modern church, she had a feeling that she should stop. She leant on the low wall, quietly looking towards the spot where Jeanne D'Arc was burned to death. Tears welled up in her eyes, and she said 'I'm so sorry Jeanne, please forgive me". She felt very calm after that.

Diana found a nearby restaurant that seemed to specialise in fish, so sat down to look at the menu.

She ordered some red wine, and a grilled fish dish then contented herself with the bread and butter provided while she waited. The square was a short way from the church of Jeanne D'Arc. Jovial music was playing in the restaurant building behind her. So different from how this place must have been at Jeanne's execution. Had Jeanne expected, even as the flames rose around her to be rescued by God? Did she feel betrayed when that didn't happen? We will never know for sure.

The fish arrived. It was tasty enough, but nothing special. Diana, deep in thought, barely noticed. A couple of local men tried to engage her in conversation, but she was well versed in evading them. Her mind was on the odd paradox of the defenders of Catholicism potentially secretly revering Pagan ideas. It surely made no sense.

She paid for her meal and left. She took a route past the cathedral's front door, the setting sun catching the stonework in bright, golden rays. She felt a tinge of sadness. Then back to her hotel to have a good night's rest. Perhaps tomorrow would provide answers.

Saturday morning arrived. Diana got up and dressed. For some reason, she decided to wear a body contoured black below the knee dress today. It was quite unusual as during digs she rarely wore anything other than T-shirts, jeans or leggings. Maybe it was a holiday mood – or perhaps it was something more profound.

Breakfast was toast, coffee and miniature croissants. Nothing special, but excellent for a hotel of this standard. As Diana drank her coffee, she pawed through the guidebook of Rouen. She would undoubtedly visit Jeanne's Tower as that had been part of Diane's château – now long since demolished. Rouen cathedral for sure, as it contained Diane's husband's tomb set into the wall.

Also, the church just outside where the château had stood, although by château the impressive artist's impression of the walls dwarfing the church fortress might have been a more appropriate description. But then Jeanne D'Arc had been imprisoned there by the English Garrison and also the Captain of Rouen – the French Steward of Normandy, had his headquarters there. The tower and the church would be the first stop. The site of Jeanne D'Arc's trial had recently been opened up for tours. It was very near to the cathedral. So the that would be the second stop.

Walking up through the narrow streets towards the Tower Diana's attention was drawn to the top of the tower as it loomed out above the low houses covering the hill - some of them replacing the château that had once stood there. It had been almost wholly obliterated over the centuries. When it had been home to Diane de Poitiers, it had been in a state of disrepair – damp, draughty, cold and unfriendly. As Diana neared the tall – rebuilt – tower she felt overwhelmed with emotion. She sat down on a nearby bench.

Suddenly I am back in a cold, dark, mediaeval scene. I am sitting alone in a large chamber. A large fireplace is filled with an intense fire, yet the room still seems 'dead', cold and oppressive. A bright but dated tapestry adorns the wall with scenes of Rouen's château in its heyday. I look down at my feet. My ankles are slim, and I am wearing light linen shoes secured with twine. My dress is thick linen in multiple layers. The majority is off-white while the top layer is the green of the forest. My wrists are narrow, and my hands are sleek and delicate with long fingers. On my wrist is a leather band with a silver crescent moon carefully secured.

I am a young woman, and I am sobbing. I hate it here. I get up from the substantial wooden chair, I tiptoe past the many rugs made from deer pelts and head up towards the base of a tower. Loose masonry chippings are evident, but I decide to climb up. My stomach is gripped by fear, the narrow spiral stairs damp with water that has seeped through the damaged roof and has washed down through the tower.

I reach the old chamber where Jeanne D'Arc had been imprisoned by the English over a century before. It has a dank, dark and cruel air to it. The only light comes through a small window with a stone ledge just big enough to sit on. I instinctively know that Jeanne had spent much of her time here. Sandwiched between the upper and lower guard quarters the small window gives a good view over the town and beyond. Yet at the same time with its solid bars and a long fall into the moat, it is also a reminder of her captivity. I carefully sit on the drier parts of the seat and imagine myself in Jeanne's position. It is here that I, and Jeanne before me, say our prayers, and we weep. I hate my time in the château here. I am happier at Anet or hunting.

Anywhere but here. "Diane!" A sharp voice echoes up the stairs. "Diane!". Sharper and louder. My husband, Louis De Brézé's voice, coming from just below me. "Diane, it is dangerous here, come back down, please. This fascination with Jeanne is not healthy. Diane!" I snap out of my daydream and hurry carefully back down the stairs. Louis' face lightens when he catches sight of me. "My love, our business will be concluded here in a few days. If you are with child, you should not take such risks. Even without you are foolish to ascend these stairs. They are unstable, and the roof is rotten. Please stay in our chamber." He is a strict but fair man, much older and shorter than me.

"Diana!" Diana stepped out of her own daydream. "Diana, what are you doing here?"

An old man had appeared beside Diana and was now addressing her. He was shabbily dressed in trousers and a waistcoat that had clearly seen better days. He had a kindly face with round glasses. It was apparent he was an academic, a man wrapped up in his studies rather than his appearance. It took a moment for Diana's composure to return. It took another moment for her to recognise him.

"Professor! Professor Schmidt. What you doing here?"

"I have a post here in Rouen, at the University. I have the chair of Medieval Studies. I'm currently Re-examining the life and death of Saint Jeanne. I often come here to ponder her life in this place where she was imprisoned. What brings you here, my child?"

"I'm researching Diane de Poitiers. As she spent much time in Rouen. It is also claimed she had a fascination with Jeanne D'Arc. Diane's name came up while I was doing a dig in the grounds of the château de Chenonceau. Amongst the ruins of the temple, we came upon a charm bracelet that may have belonged to her. Ever since her name has been inextricably linked to my dig, so I decided to take some time out and look around Rouen. She lived in the château here, while her husband has a tomb that she had built for him in the cathedral. Are you familiar with her?"

"Why yes, of course. Diane de Poitiers is woven into the Renaissance story here. She was the wife of Louis De Brézé, the Steward of Normandy. It was the French equivalent to the Duke of Normandy, but that title, of course, belonged to the English

King. On his death, she effectively assumed his duties. She was quite a remarkable woman. I can happily show you around. The conference I was hoping to attend this weekend has been cancelled, so I'm entirely at your service. But I'm sure that a young man must be meeting with you here?"

"No. I'm on my own. My assistant is away at his Parents. I'm single. Your offer would be fantastic, and so helpful. Will you show me around the château ruins and the other sites here in Rouen?"

"Sure."

"Thank you."

"Let's start with the tower here. Mind the steps. Many people wrongly believed that Saint Jeanne was imprisoned in the roof, but in actual fact, she was held on the first floor. That avoided her climbing the rafters and loosening the tiles or making a run for it. So, she was actually between an upper and a lower guardhouse. That was much more effective."

The professor ushered Diana up to the first floor via the spiral stairs. Diana disliked spiral stairs but took deep breaths to allow her to climb up.

"This is the place where Joan could view the city of Rouen. She could peer through the bars at the English Garrison, smell the air, but could not be part of it. There is an almost indiscernible cross barely visible here. I almost imagine Joan scratching it in with her nails to symbolise her faith and devotion."

"That is amazing. Do you think Diane de Poitiers would have come here?"

"Almost certainly. Diane would have been privy to the prior layout of the fortress from her husband, the Steward. But this part was in a bad state of repair by her time. The stairs would have been dank and treacherous by her time as the roof was party missing and this whole wing was abandoned after the English left. Louis De Brézé and the other stewards did not want to spend money on this old place as it had come to symbolise the English rule here, so was largely hated by the French. It just made a useful stronghold if required for the Captain of Rouen, as Louis also was. The sleeping quarters were rudimentary but habitable in the Renaissance period."

"Interesting." Diana felt compelled to sit down in the seat by the window. She was briefly transported to a dank and draughty vista. It was the same view over the city, but the scene was mediaeval with palls of smoke lingering over tumbledown houses, the noise of bells from several churches ringing nearby.

"Come, shall we go on up?" Diana was brought out of her trance as the Professor gestured for her to follow him up the stairs.

After some more stairs, a breathless Diana was in the top of the tower beneath a conical wooden roof. She was breathless through her fear of the spiral stairs rather than being unfit. The Professor continued his tour guide spiel.

"So, this is the upper guardhouse. In Joan's time, the men who lived here would have been charged with preventing her escape. The concrete here is not original. The NAZI occupiers rebuilt and fortified this area as a bomb-proof bunker against Allied bombing. In the 1940s this was a lookout and command post again occupied by troops of a foreign Garrison. Perhaps the French should have completed the demolition after all."

"No. I'm glad it was kept. There are still reminders of Jeanne D'Arc here."

"Quite so. It is a marvel to have this small glimpse of a once-great bastion. Where would you like to go next?"

"I'm not sure – the cathedral?"

"No. I have a better idea. I'll take you to the Garrison's local church. It was outside the château walls and still stands. I'll drop into the Rector's house for the key en route as the building is locked mostly these days."

"That would be most interesting thank you."

A thin man living in a modest house nearby exchanged pleasantries with the Professor before disappearing and reappearing with a large rusty key.

"Merci".

"Let's go to church. I'm sure you will be fascinated. At least one of Diane De Poitiers' children was baptised here during one of her many stays in her husband's time."

"Great."

The church was uninspiring from the outside. The massive outside door was scruffy, its lock rusted and stiff. The Professor struggled to unlock and open it. Eventually, it yielded, and the archaeologists were given a view inside. It was gloomy and the air inside smelt musty. It was obviously old and underused. Wandering inside, Diana glanced around at the plain décor of the walls. There were some plaques relating to the various Captains of Rouen – occasionally ornate, but none that inspiring. The altar was also low key – a blue with a gold trim altar cloth, a pair of large candles and a silver crucifix in the centre. Yet it had some familiarity to it…

Heinz spoke. "Your friend Diane would have come here often. As a high-born woman attending with her husband, she would have been able to sit near the front. Formal segregation such as at cathedrals would not have applied here the same way. It was really just a large castle chapel. An account exists of a wedding of one of Louis De Brézé's loyal lieutenants. It mentions that the bride wore her best dress, her husband his finest uniform while his master wore his formal attire as Captain of Rouen and Seneschal of Normandie. Diane De Poitiers' wore her finest green silk dress for the occasion, the account noted."

Diana nodded at this. It seemed to ring true for her, but her attention was drawn to the font. She had to go over and look at it. It was very worn and obviously the original mediaeval piece. She leant over to touch it. Her senses slowed, propelling her into another world...

I am holding a baby. A baby girl. A very young baby who is only a few weeks old. The priest, a very austere man, is speaking quickly in Latin. My view is obscured by a covering over my face – a full veil. The Priest looks towards me, so I hand my baby to him. He holds the baby aloft, then lowers her towards the font. The font is in pristine condition – polished alabaster with crisp Christian symbols around the rim.

He cups his hand and scoops up a handful of the blessed water, pours it on the baby's face, then draws the sign of the cross while he mixes Latin with the child's name Louise Marie De Brézé. My baby girl is crying as the priest passes her back to me - her mother. Looking down at my child, I can see the pale skin of my baby's face, plump and with a wisp of orange-blonde hair – like my own. This is the christening of my youngest daughter Louise in the church of Rouen.

Looking down I am wearing an elegant but straightforward dress in green with some taffeta trim. My figure is still quite trim despite my pregnancy and birth. I am The Huntress in my maternal, nurturing form, soothing and comforting my crying daughter. There are potent smells of incense, men's sweat and baby urine along with bright sunshine streaming through the clean and clear church windows. Cheers come up from Louis' men after the ceremony. Our family are loved and respected by Louis' men.

A sharp cough broke the spell and brought Diana back to the present day.

"Are you alright, Diana?" The professor's voice showed more than just a little concern for the woman he was showing around.

"Ah, I'm, I'm just having a bit of a daydream. I'm sure so many events must have taken place here."

"I'm sure you're right, but many records have been lost over the centuries. It is sad, but we have to let go sometimes. Do you need to sit down?"

"No, I'll be fine, thank you."

"Great. Shall we move on?"

"Yes, let's do that."

The Archaeologists moved on briskly towards the cathedral in Rouen. The asymmetric towers gave the building a different feel to many other cathedrals, one tower seemingly very delicate compared to those elsewhere and adjacent. The bright square in front of the cathedral allowed an uncluttered view of the doors into the structure. The ornate door surrounds with their medieval carvings had been recently cleaned and showed their original crispness and delicate sandstone hues in the morning sunlight.

As Heinz showed Diana through the left-hand door, she felt a tinge of sadness on entering.

The pair strolled towards the altar in near silence, with Diana thoroughly looking up and down the walls between the stained-glass windows and the side chapels. She was looking for Louis De Brézé's tomb – a beautiful piece of Renaissance carving designed for and paid for by Diane de Poitiers. But although Diana had seen many excellent pictures of it, she did not know how big it was, nor where it was on the walls within the cathedral. She peered into the gated area of the main altar, then as she turned to start walking back down the right side of the nave, a sickening feeling gripped her – she had gone past the tomb! But how?

"We must stop Professor. I think we have gone past."

"I will ask. Stay here."

A few moments later, Heinz returned with one of the church supervisors.

"Hello, how may I help?" said the thick-set man with glasses. He was in his fifties and was wearing a crumpled suit.

"I'm looking for the tomb of Louis De Brézé, please. But I can't see it here."

"But Mademoiselle it is behind you, behind these gates, on the left-hand wall towards the altar. You know Louis De Brézé was the husband of Diane de Poitiers – long before she was Henri the second's mistress. She paid for it to be built and for its upkeep. Come with me, and I'll show it to you, and where Diane must have sat on her many visits here between its construction and her own death."

"Thank you so much, Monsieur."

"Du Puis. Luc Du Puis. And you would be?"

"I'm Doctor Diana Garry, and this is an old colleague of mine, Professor Heinz Schmidt. We're both well acquainted with Diane de Poitiers, but I have not been here before." Replied Diana.

"That is strange. You seem very familiar Madame." The man took a more formal tone. "What field of study are you in?"

"We're Archaeologists. I'm involved in a dig at the Château of Chenonceau."

"Chenonceau, fascinating. A dig at an intact château. Please explain."

Du Puis was tightly gripping his key to the altar area. He seemed slightly alarmed.

"My current dig is on a Roman temple in the grounds at Chenonceau, but we discovered an artefact that belonged to Diane de Poitiers. Since then, I've been visiting sites relating to Diane, partly in my own time, like today. She was a fascinating woman."

Luc relaxed during Diana's reply and started to unlock the gate as soon as she'd finished.

"Indeed. Come and see another piece of your jigsaw puzzle. Some of the imagery is still enigmatic. But Diane was fond of Louis. It shows."

"Yes, you can use your camera, here's my card if you wish to contact me later. Any fresh insights are always welcome. Our guide book is due to be updated, and the information on this magnificent tomb is still incomplete. The animals at the top are very unusual. A lamb perhaps, but why a goat too?" He pointed to the small detail on the right.

The tomb was very intricate with details of Louis De Brézé on a horse in life, as well as in death below. Although no more than three to four metres high and nearly as wide it was exquisite with its many carvings. In the sixteenth century, it must have cost a pretty penny.

"May I touch it?"

"Of course. I'm sure that Louis would have approved."

Diana was drawn to the carvings of Louis. Black marble. Cold to the touch but sharp and well defined. She felt tears welling up inside her. "Oh, Louis!" she whispered.

The Professor gave her a strange look.

"Immersive history Diana, but be careful. It was a defining yet turbulent era. Diane de Poitiers was a feisty character. As controversial as Eva Peron in her day."

Diana finished running her fingers over the casting, then took a small handkerchief out from her handbag before putting it to her cheek to soak up the tears.

"I feel strangely connected to this place, to the château, to this woman and those in her life."

Diana nodded towards the mausoleum.

"As an academic, with my training, from my use of scientific methods, it seems madness. Yet as a woman, my deepest instincts and intuition tell me otherwise. I've had too much déjà vu these past few weeks and months. Ever since I arrived at Chenonceaux, things have been happening. Could it be possible?"

Diana struggled to vocalise her thoughts to an academic peer.

"Forgive me, but do you think it is possible. Can reincarnation be possible?"

The professor took a sharp intake of breath.

"Yes, I believe it is possible. But I did not always believe it to be so. As you may remember a couple of years ago - when we first met- the body of an English King – Richard the third – was recovered from a car park in the city of Leicester. We were observers there at the time. I saw with my own eyes a woman pointing at the letter "R" on a parking space saying 'dig here'. A short while later a curved spine skeleton was recovered. Subsequently, DNA showed it was Richard. I believe that she had a strong link to one of Richard's esquires or perhaps Richard himself. Her knowledge was too precise, too exact, too extensive to be from research – much of the documents anti-Richard propaganda."

He turned to look into Diana's eyes.

"And another time, in Germany, a boy in my home village

located the body of his past self from a lake. He had been having nightmares about a fighter pilot who had been attacking bombers flying over Germany during world war two, before a dogfight critically damaged his aircraft, causing it to catch fire. The boy screamed as he recalled burning in the fire in his cockpit, before a rush of water that extinguished the fire and his life. "

"That boy grew up with a fear of naked flames and of drowning. He also hated wearing seatbelts. But one day, in a nightmare, he was drawn to a nearby lake. Grabbing a map, he pinpointed the position. His parents didn't believe him, but his Uncle did. A keen diver with a boat, the uncle, took the boy with him out to the lake, out to where the boy said the plane went down. He dived down, and, through a plume of mud particles, he saw the dark outline of a Messerschmitt BF 109 E fighter."

"There, still in the cockpit, was the body – by now a skeleton – still strapped into the rusting fuselage. The plane still had the squadron insignia and ID plate in place. The letters TK 105 identified it as squadron leader Otto Von Schultz, who was lost in action late in September 1943. The boy's uncle deployed a marker buoy over the wreck site. The next day the boy returned in the boat with his parents to lay a wreath and say a prayer at the site. The boy was in floods of tears. But he also felt great joy and closure. He never had those nightmares ever again."

Diana's mouth fell open at that last piece of the story.

"So, you may ask 'Why is he telling me this story?'"

"Well, yes actually," said a confused Diana

"Well. I was that boy. And I have never shared the story to anyone outside of my family. I had also suppressed it for a long time afterwards."

"Thank you, Heinz. It means a lot to me. So, perhaps, I was Diane. Or someone connected to her?"

"Precisely. Trust your intuition. Trust it."

The two Archaeologists looked through the souvenir shop before they left, dropping back the key to the altar section and to chief guide there. Diana purchased a couple of postcards to send on to her parents and sisters.

Outside the smell of fresh brioche enticed Diana to invite the professor for a snack at a local patisserie and café. A warm brioche slice with butter and strawberry jam next to a piping hot cup of black coffee opposite to Heinz Schmitt's mug of lemon tea and Danish pastry sat between them as Heinz next spoke.

"Diana, there is one last place you should visit. It is the site of the inquisition court that sat in judgment of Joan of Arc at her trial here in Rouen. It has only recently been refurbished and opened to the public. I think you will find it interesting."

"Thank you, Heinz. It is so great to have you show me the sights here. It would have taken a lot longer to find and visit them without you."

Down a side street next to the cathedral was a somewhat touristic 'Joan of Arc Experience'. The pair bought tickets and were given headsets to wear as they waited for a tour guide to usher them round. Diana felt great trepidation at entering the building. It was a complex of rooms and halls overlooking a courtyard that belonged to the church authorities. At the time of Jeanne's trial, several pro-English religious clerics were brought in to ensure a swift and convenient end was put to the Maid of Orleans, regardless of her testimony.

In the main trial hall, the visitors were treated to a projected reconstruction of the trial scene. Jeanne gave an impassioned defence of her visions and actions, but to no avail against a biased court. The verdict was inevitable. As the proceedings went on, Diana found herself weeping. It was a profound experience for her. She felt a deep sense of regret, an affinity for Jeanne and somehow responsibility for this young girl facing trial. As the verdict was read out, she was inconsolable.

The professor patted her shoulders gently.

“I think we should go out and get some fresh air, Diana.”

“Thank you, Heinz.”

After leaving the site of the trial, Diana brightened up considerably.

“I have no idea what that was about. I’ve always been interested in Jeanne’s story. But why would I feel responsible for her fate? It makes no sense.”

“That I cannot explain. It may always remain a mystery. But certainly, there are many views that Jeanne had been sought out by powerful supporters of the exiled Dauphin. He had been weak and indecisive before she came to him. Perhaps... Just perhaps... You were somehow one of them back then. If we can live more than once, then why not more than twice. All I can suggest is that you forgive yourself for your part if you had one.”

“Okay. I will Heinz.”

“A friend of mine – a spiritual soul – sends herself ‘Ho'oponopono’ – which she finds helpful. We’re the most critical critics of ourselves. Perhaps that criticism and guilt transcend time and lifetimes.”

“Thank you. I’ll look into it.”

The rest of the day was pleasant but uneventful for Diana. After a final meal with Heinz, Diana returned to her hotel room. In no mood for socialising she decided to write up and notes on her visit to Rouen. She also looked up ‘Ho'oponopono’.

“Fascinating.” She said herself.

“I love you; I forgive you, I’m sorry, thank you.” She said

the words of the Hawaiian forgiveness mantra to herself as she consciously thought of Jeanne D'Arc and her allies. Diana slept a peaceful sleep that night.

The next morning, she ate the small croissants provided for breakfast over a couple of mugs of steaming coffee.

That done, she returned to her room, packed then checked out. In her car, she muttered.

"Right, back to Chenonceau."

XXI - The Ring

Back in Chenonceau Diana Garry was at her desk. The mug of coffee in front of her untouched, its cooling surface still giving off small puffs of steam. In her hand in front of her face, a little plastic zip-up pouch containing the bracelet purported to have belonged to Diane de Poitiers. Diana's gaze was fixed on the Crescent moon as her assistant Stan shuffled in and gave a short cough as he stood before her. As she looked up towards him, for a moment, just a moment, his features took on a more rugged yet majestic shape before settling back into Stan's face. She whispered quietly to herself "Henri, Mon Coeur".

"Uh, sorry?" Stan frowned at his boss as she stuttered and started.

"S…S…Sorry Stan. Things on my mind. I hear there's been a significant find?"

"Yes, Diana. But not from our favourite period. This one is mediaeval, well Renaissance era. It's a ring that was again placed within the ruins of our temple to Diana. Just the side of the lunarium. It is in great condition. It seems that it was buried inside a strong leather pouch. It is small, so a woman's ring. The banding is exquisite - gold and silver intertwined, with a motif of three intertwined crescent moons on the top, with a monogram of a stylised 'H' and 'D'. Let's face it, this ring must have belonged to Henri the second's Mistress Diane de Poitiers.

The design is far too distinctive to be otherwise. It's quite a find."

Diana was dumbstruck. She had picked up the ring.

Instantly I am back in time at the occasion when Henri gave me the ring. It has been a few weeks after I had lost a similar ring that was one of a pair that we as a couple had both worn as an unofficial wedding ring. As an active and busy woman, I have somehow completely lost the ring while out hunting. And it can just not be found. The ring that Henri presents to me is very similar but more ornate than the original.

Henri presents the ring to me while in my bedchamber at Chenonceau. Amidst the heavy burgundy bed sheets and blankets over the delicate silk sheets, he hands me the monogrammed leather pouch in black with silver lettering embossed on it. I take it, loosening the leather ties to reveal the ring inside. I lift it up to the dim morning light of autumn to reveal its delicate pattern.

I say "Oh, Mon Coeur, c'est magnifique."

I slipped it on to my delicate ring finger, then embrace and kiss him. Tears well up in my eyes.

"It is so beautiful, my love."

The image faded as she gazed into Stan's eyes. Momentarily his eyes were those of Henri.

"I'm amazed that we have found such a thing here that has been deliberately hidden in amongst the ruins of the temple. What is going on here, Stan?"

"I don't know Diana. We have always believed that such knowledge of the Roman era was lost in the dark ages. Yet we have Renaissance artefacts bearing a lunar motif deliberately placed in the ruins of a temple dedicated to the moon goddess Diana. It seems our belief may be flawed."

"Indeed. The French royals before Charlemagne did appear to

mark pagan sites within Paris, particularly with special respect. Henri II and Diane traced their ancestry back to those royals. Were that respect and knowledge passed down within the royal lineage?"

Stan shrugged his shoulders at this.

"Perhaps. Or perhaps we've read too much into a series of coincidences."

"How do you suggest we proceed? We have significant finds out of place but placed in inclusion datable to the late Mediaeval or Renaissance era. The artefacts are attributable to Diane de Poitiers but are unlikely to have been left by the lady herself. Who are the likely suspects to have left them?"

Stan smiled before replying. "Her daughters. She had two of them. Francoise and Louise. We should concentrate on then."

"Well actually, I believe she had a third daughter. Diane de France."

"As I recall she was Henri's daughter by another mistress. Not Diane's."

"I believe differently. Diane de France closely resembled Diane de Poitiers and was closely supervised by her. It never makes any sense except in the context of her being Diane's own daughter."

"You have a point." Stan nodded. "And as a royal child, she would have greater access to Chenonceau than Diane de Poitiers' legitimate daughters."

Diana carried on with her line of thinking. "If Diane De France had been Diane's natural daughter and that of Henri's, then she would have been the prime candidate to inherit her mother's love charms. We should chase up any known documents on Diane De France. They would be part of the royal archives if we're lucky and they have avoided destruction."

Diana Garry spent much of the next few days cataloguing finds, visiting the dig sites and calling around the various archives of royal and governmental documents within France for more facts on both Dianes. The Terreur had accounted for many sources, but not all. Although letters and account books were in private collections some copies of originals were in museums and town halls across France. One such example was at the Parisian school of jewellery. A disputed bill between a Monsieur D'Argent and Diane De France itemised some jewellery sent for cleaning by Diane junior.

One piece was described as 'My mother's ring. Interleaved gold and silver band with three crescent moons interlocked.' The bill was dated February 1568. This appeared to confirm that the ring found at Chenonceau had indeed passed into the possession of Diane De France. It also (controversially) seemed to confirm that Diane de Poitiers was considered to be her mother or actually was her mother. It was like gold dust. The mood in Diana's Office lightened considerably. But the mystery remained of how and why such a treasured possession should be deposited in the grounds of Chenonceau. That was still was a mystery.

On Friday afternoon Diana Garry was drinking her third coffee of the day while she pondered the mystery. A flash of inspiration crossed her mind.

"Stan!" Dr Garry had leapt to her feet and opened the connecting door into her assistant's modest office. She sighed at his X-Files calendar and his collection of Star Wars miniatures on a small shelf above his Archaeology reference books.

"What is it, boss? What's up?"

"I'm just kicking myself. We may have all the answers here at Chenonceau. Do we still have access to the archives here?"

"Yes, of course. Most are on microfiche here." Stan gestured towards an old microfiche reader and a wooden box on top of it at the edge of his desk. He blew the dust off the top of both before lifting the box on to the centre of his reading desk.

"What are you thinking of? We've been through the inventories and account records. What have we missed?"

"The guest lists. Chenonceau hosted many parties during Catherine De Medici's time. I think we should look for attendance of Diane De France here after 1566. She was likely invited. And her entourage may give us a final clue."

"OK. Let's do it. It will give me a break from cataloguing broken tiles we've found."

After a couple of hours of searching, the party to honour the Hungarian ambassador in 1568, was settled upon. Diane of France and her valets attended. It was the start. She would have been free to wander the grounds with her servants or perhaps passed on the items to the château gardeners and servants, some of whom had been fond of Diane de Poitiers. It would be almost impossible to prove beyond a reasonable doubt. But at the same time, it was possible, and it was plausible.

Diana remained thoughtful and optimistic about investigations into the out of place artefacts. She resumed work on examining the layout of the temple to her namesake goddess. From previous excavations, a central feature was a beautiful mosaic floor in the centre of the temple. From small pieces of tessali already recovered, and from the geophysics survey recently completed, she had a good idea where this was located. She had discussed this with the château, and they had given her their permission to uncover the section in the far corner of what was called Diane de Poitiers' Garden. As it was now Autumn and the roses and other shrubs could be lifted out carefully and placed in a holding area while the dig took place. The team of archaeological students from Nice had been drafted in for this phase to assist in digging and sifting the many tonnes of soil that would need to be disturbed.

Stan took with relish to flying the team's new toy – a drone. The drone was fitted with infrared and ultraviolet sensitive cameras so was able to note any land features unseen by the naked eye. The dryer area in the vicinity of the temple indicated a lot of intact structure underneath. The surveyors, including Diana, set out the site perimeter, and a small digger was committed to digging out the first metre or so of alluvial clay and shingle laid down by the river as it had tried to reclaim the site every flood season between the temple's disuse and the building of the retaining wall in the renaissance era. Thankfully, the wall had barely clipped the edges of the temple ruin.

Diana caught Stan admiring more than just the view as the many twenty-year-old female students stripped down to their tank tops and bikini tops as they warmed up with the effort of digging.

"How's it going, Stan?" Diana coughed to get her assistant's attention.

"Uh, hi, Diana. I'm just observing the lie of the land."

"I don't doubt you're observing, Stan. Just don't disturb something you shouldn't!"

"Oh. Those girls are too young for me. I'm not that energetic anymore."

Diana smiled.

As the digger completed its task, the students got to work digging out more carefully through the remaining layers of soil. Depth gauge pictures were taken as soon as a piece of wall was struck. The waste piles from the digger were sifted for finds. It soon yielded a host of lost centimes, Euro cents and assorted modern era debris as well as a lovely brooch and gold ring from the intervening years since the garden was built. Quite a lot of broken pipe stems and bowls stood testament to the efforts of the gardeners in preserving the legacy of Diane's garden.

It was towards late afternoon as the autumnal lighting and moved nearer to sunset when a shout rang out from a young woman in the middle of the dig site. She shouted out "Regard, tessali, vite, vite!"

Amelie, a young woman from Lyons, was gesturing wildly and pointing below her feet. She had just used a damp sponge to expose a section of flooring some 30 cm square. Diana and Stan rushed over to take a look. Staring back at them was the unmistakable side of the man's face, exquisitely detailed in the tiniest tessali.

"C'est magnifique!" A number at the other diggers gasped as they saw the sight.

Diana looked down at the tiles, then back up at Stan, back and forth three or four times as she gasped "No. It can't be!"

"What's wrong, Diana?" Queried Stan.

"Look, Stan. It's a male portrait. It's in the middle of a temple of Diana. And facially it bears more than just a passing resemblance to you! How many more surprises can I take? This isn't the deity we were expecting. Have we unearthed the wrong temple?"

"But Diana. You should be pleased, this is an amazing discovery. Get a grip, please."

"I guess you're right. I've been too hard on myself. And on you. And the others. Let's carefully dig outwards and see what we have. The context is everything."

Diana herself stepped down into the pit, rolled up her sleeves, tied her hair back and picked up a nearby scraper and paintbrush. She had a determined look on her face.

"The male figure - Apollo? Is facing right, looking towards

someone or something. What is that something?"

"Atta girl. Stay positive. Stan meant to be supportive but...

"Don't. I'm not seventeen Stan. It's my dig."

Dusk fell, and so did the night. The sounds of woodland creatures echoed from beyond the retaining wall and from the other side of the Cher river. The gurgling of the water interspersed with metallic scraping and brushing noises. At around 9 o'clock a hopeful area a short distance to the left of the male portrait was sponged down to reveal...a mirror portrait of the Huntress. Dark hair with a crescent moon tiara and dark brown eyes in the finest quality tessali.

The floodlights with their harsh white light diminished none of the beauty of the portrait of Diana – Artemis - the patron goddess of the temple being dug. But again, the features of the picture looked uncannily likes Diana Garry, and yet in their perfection also very much like Diane de Poitiers. Neither was lost on any of those assembled peering down upon the portrait. Diana sat down, shaking her head.

"This just can't be. Coincidence doesn't come close. The press are bound to draw parallels with us, Stan. We will need to speak to Paris, tell the château owners and release a press release. I feel a bad hair day coming up for you and me Stan. Let's make sure we look less than perfect for the press. The Diane de Poitiers' link we can live with."

"Agreed, Diana. I think we need to post guards on the site from now on."

"Yes."

Stan and two other men from the combined dig team took four-hour shifts during that night to ensure the site remained untouched. It was agreed that in the morning the château security team and management would be alerted.

Diana had retired to the dig's favourite bar in a hotel across the road in the town, just a comfortable walk from the château. The youngsters were beaming at their success on their first significant dig. Yet Diana was genuinely conflicted. She knew that such a find would have far-reaching consequences. In short, it put her excavation firmly on the map and in the public eye.

Her maverick father would have loved the platform it opened up, but she wasn't her father. A significant mosaic at a site was the archaeological equivalent of making a hit record. The five minutes of fame could make or break her career. And with a tiled pavement that featured mythological characters who looked just like the chief diggers, the press could have a field day.

So it was with trepidation that Diana greeted Stan when he arrived back after his shift on-site for a last drink at the bar.

"Hi, Diana. I'm surprised you're not in bed by now."

"I know." Diana gave in to her worst temptation and lit up a Gauloises. She was visibly shaking.

"This is great for the dig, for the team and for the château. But you saw the portraits. How the hell can we explain those away? I fully intend to wear my hair up and wear my glasses throughout any press conferences we attend. I suggest you cultivate your goatee and wear those polo necks you are so fond of. We might just get away with it as long as they don't pull out stock photos. I've already alerted mum about press intrusion. You might want to alert your family too."

"OK. But I honestly doubt the Press will notice. We should have time to plan while we dig out the rest of the tiles."

"That's true. And if we happen upon the best Diane de Poitiers' portrait to match with the goddess figure, we may take the heat off of us."

"Good idea. The château will like that. It's a temple to Diana in Diane's Garden discovered by Diana."

"OK - except that last bit!"

XXII - Publicity

"Magnificent mosaic to Diana found in Diane's garden at château."

That was the headline that resulted from a press conference held jointly by the French Ministry of Antiquities, the universities and the château of Chenonceau.

Dr Diana Garry and her team conducted themselves well. Diana dressed a little bit down for the occasion, along with unflattering glasses, while Stan complimented his look with the spectacles he usually hated to wear. With her hair tied up at the back, the pair looked as far removed from the god and goddess depicted in the mosaic as it was possible to be. They posed for copious amounts of pictures for the press - both fastidiously refusing to remove their glasses.

The director of antiquities and the châteaux owners were both pleased with the outcome. The expected increase in tourism would balance out the need for more on-site security. Even the potential to display the mosaic underneath a perspex casing amongst the garden's flower bed was agreed in principle, with a 'finds room' being earmarked for one of the stable blocks to be opened for the following summer.

Relaxed and relieved Diana invited Stan for a celebration meal at her favourite bistro in the town. He readily agreed.

With every course, the pair were enjoying a couple of shots of pastis. The previous tension and stress now are gone. The duck pâte slid down nicely, the quail and oysters similarly so. Laughs and tales of their youth and at other digs filling the air with joy. It was evident from any observers that a certain chemistry existed between the two, but had never been vocalised by either. The bar was emptying when Stan had leaned over to Diana and whispered in her ear. "I have pastis in my room - why not come up?"

"OK." Replied Diana.

The pair were soon leaning on each other as they stumbled up towards Stan's room in a nearby apartment in the town. Stan haphazardly removed his key from his pocket and at the third attempt managed to get it into the lock and turn it. The room was sparse, with a strong musky odour of single man about it, where the window had been shut all day.

Stan turned on the light switch to reveal a bottle of pastis on his dresser – shot glasses piled next to it. He went towards the bottle, but Diana held him back. She pulled him towards her and caressed his face and goatee beard before leaning in on him and planting a firm kiss on his lips. He, in turn, relaxed his arms, puckered up his lips and moved to embrace her warm body.

"I want you," she said.

"I know. And I want you too," Said he.

"I thought you did," she replied.

They both giggled before fully embracing each other in their spontaneous release of passion.

The embrace lasted for several minutes in the dim light of Stan's apartment. The evident passion, coupled with Stan's firm embrace on Diana's warm, supple body, could only end one way. Angling his arm down towards her buttocks, Stan lifted Diana into his arms before carrying her into his bedroom. He lifted her onto his roughly made double bed, the couple quickly throwing the contents on to the floor as they were getting into the throes of passion.

Stan fumbled for the zip of Diana's burgundy dress. With a tug, the zip was undone, with a pull the fabric sailed over her head, over the bed and on to the floor. Luckily for Diana, she had just changed into nice, flattering lingerie in a matching hue. He then assisted Diana in undoing his rugby shirt and hurling it onto the floor. His muscular chest and mat of ginger-brown chest hair contrasting with Diana's toned and trim body in the dim light of Stan's bedroom.

Diana was noticeably trembling as he ran his hands down her sides to her narrow waist. She leant out to caress his firm, hairy chest. Struggling at first with the clasp, Stan undid her bra, letting it fall forward slowly to reveal her modest yet firm breasts. He traced her figure with his hands, softly caressing her soft, curvy form with his fingers. As he did so, she shivered and broke out in goosebumps all over. She leaned forward, and they embraced once again. The force did momentarily knock her left nipple, causing her to yelp.

Stan asked, "Are you sure?" Diana eagerly nodded.

They hungrily embraced and kissed deeply, as if they had waited all their lives for this moment – or maybe many lifetimes. They were ecstatic in their moment.

Fully aroused in their passion, they let go of their embrace to take off their bottoms. A pair of trousers, pants and lovely lingerie all gravitated to the floor as momentum propelled them onwards.

Their pent-up lust consumed them. A lifetime of longing – maybe longer - was unleashed as the lovers embraced in a physical act of union. Their unrequited passion consumed them, keeping them in a series of passionate unions all night long, with caution thrown to the winds.

After their lovemaking, Diana fell into a deep sleep and once again had a dream...

It was inevitable. My regular lovemaking with Henri leads to its possible conclusion. I have missed periods, morning sickness and dizziness. As an experienced midwife and mother of two, I know that I am pregnant. I feel the sickness, queasiness and dizziness in myself. I take a Rosemary and Fennell herbal cure for my morning sickness. I tell Henri "Mon Coeur – I am with child – our child". Henri is overcome with joy, kissing me and patting my tummy.

He says "But I'm going away soon – will you be alright?"

I reply "I will be fine, my love. But..."

"But what my love?" he asks.

I reply "There will be a scandal at court if this becomes known. We must keep this secret, and soon I will have to leave court."

He counters "But I want my child – our child – at court."

I say "You will my sweet. I have a plan. I will feign 'Malaise Italien' [a contagious disease associated with the wars in Italy] *from you, leave court, and keep only my most loyal staff with me at Anet. You must take a mistress while on your campaign in Piedmont and put her with child. She must be pretty – but not too beautiful!* Charles [the squire who had accompanied Diane to her Father's prison years before] *will organise the rest – with your blessing?"*

He replies "Of course, my love. But it will pain me greatly to lay with another as our love ripens within you."

I confirm "It must be so. We have enemies at Court."

I am pregnant. However, I see to it that there is not to be a rival child from Filippa Duci. Charles is able to put a mild dose of belladonna into the girl's drink some months into her pregnancy. She becomes feverish. She is taken amid great secrecy to a nearby convent where she loses her child. She is kept confined – the loss of her child is kept a secret.

I give birth to 'Petite Diane' on 14th February 1538, around seven in the morning with just my most trusted maids present. It was (luckily) a straightforward birth for me.

Sometime later one of my squires, whose wife had given birth to a daughter shortly after me, travel out with his wife (and his daughter, secretly) to Henri's camp and the convent. His wife acts as 'nurse' for Henri's daughter.

My squire's daughter works her part.

Henri, Charles and the squire's family return to Anet, where our child is substituted. It is a wrench to give up my daughter this way, but it is necessary. I am now recovered after vigorous exercise which I have abstained from during my pregnancy (except for swimming) – take on the responsibility for Henri's daughter. Henri insists she is called 'Diane'. We all return to Court – much to the annoyance of my enemy Anne de Pisseleu (King Francis I's mistress) and Henri's wife, Catherine.

As dawn broke, the two lovers were awakened by a fierce thunderstorm rumbling in the near distance. As the lightning flashed the faces of the two lovers were lit up to show utter contentment and satisfaction.

Over a meagre breakfast of toast and coffee in Stan's rooms, the couple barely spoke. It was somewhat surreal. Two beings out of time had met up again to rekindle their love. This time neither wanting to lose the other again.

In the end, Diana broke the silence as she dressed in her clothes from the previous night.

"I have to go. But it was great. We will need to assess the situation when the dust settles, but it can be worked out. Are you OK?"

"Of course, my love. I guess we'll have to see how it affects our working relationship. But we can sort it out. See you later."

They hugged and kissed before Diana returned to her own room to change ready for a new working day.

XXIII - Fate

Back at the office, the director of Chenonceau was waiting for Diana when she arrived.

"Ah, Diana. Bon. We must consider our options with the care and display of our splendid Roman pavement.

We would very much like to display it of course, but sympathetically to the site and to Diane's garden."

"Of course, Monsieur director. I have already made contact with other Roman sites with similar mosaics. We have many options on display and presentation. But first, with your permission, we wish to excavate around the edges of the site to mark out its full extent so that any glass flooring over the tessali does not damage the temple structure. I have requested geophysics use ground-penetrating radar at the maximum resolution as a first step before we request more of the site to dig via the detailed ground maps."

"That sounds quite satisfactory, Diana. Please keep me abreast of developments."

"Of course, director. My superiors in Paris are also being kept up on all events."

The director nodded, saying a few 'Bon's' while he stood looking carefully at Diane's face.

"It is remarkable that the effigy of the goddess bears not only a passing resemblance to Diane de Poitiers but an even more striking one to yourself. An amazing coincidence do you not think, Diana?"

Diana flushed behind her thin layer of foundation. She hoped it didn't show too obviously.

"Oh, do you think so? I hadn't really noticed. I suspect it's more down to my age and colouring. A mere coincidence. You'll be saying that the god looks like Stan next!"

As soon as she had said it, she regretted it. The director frowned and then smiled.

"Actually, now that you mention it, he does. And to Diane's love, Henri II. Fate has a strong hand here. You will forever be linked to this find, this mosaic, this site, Diane's garden, Chenonceau and all of its ghosts. Remarkable indeed."

He smiled, bowed and left.

"Au revoir, Diana," he said on parting, with a big smile on his face.

"Merde," said Diana under her breath once alone.

Diana poured herself another coffee and took it with her to the adjacent room. Stan was just taking off his jacket as she opened the door.

"Hi, Diana! I didn't expect to see you so soon today," he smiled, then became more serious as he realised, she was looking agitated.

"Hi, Stan. Yes, the château director was just here earlier. He did indeed remark on my likeness to the mosaic's goddess portrait, then I blurted out your likeness, and he agreed with that too. He's right. We're both linked to here forever. The curse for archaeologists."

"This could be the making of you. Don't worry. Not everybody puts us into boxes. Besides, it's a Roman find. Not out of place, not Renaissance. It's your speciality oh dig director from Roman Bath Sulis. Your notoriety and chances of funding have just gone up overnight. You will be offered amazing opportunities you could never have imagined a few days or weeks ago. In fact, isn't that the telegram guy now?"

"Who sends telegrams these days?"

They both sighed and said in unison "Paris."

It was true. Diane signed for the envelope, then quickly tore it open. She read it aloud.

"Madame Director. You are hereby invited to the Ministry of Antiquities in Paris to give a full explanation of your find to the minister, and as part of a private visit, you will accompany him to on a tour of a recent startling find on the banks of the Seine. Please arrive at the ministry tomorrow morning at 09:00 prompt."

"Sacre bleu. There you see!" Said Stan.

That night Diane had a troubled sleep before falling into another dream...

It is Henri's Coronation and his triumphal entrance into Paris on 25th July 1457. I am wearing my most iconic dress (later captured in my favourite portrait) – it is beautiful – a dressmaker from Milan was brought in specially to assist in making it for me. It is black velvet with silver threaded, full length, embroidery and pattern all over the dress, bodice and skirt. No expense has been spared. I wear matching shoes of black velvet and soft leather with wooden soles.

I ride my best white horse with a braided mane and tail. I ride towards the front of the parade, but I am on my own. There are cheering crowds and a broad thoroughfare. We ride at a slow pace; I smell the pungent smells of the different districts on the route -

not always pleasant! Black and silver banners are present with our 'HD' motif. I witness pride, happiness and strongly joyful feelings amongst the people. I wave to the crowd, who mainly cheer for me.

In the cathedral, with its tall roof, we all sit in our raised boxes. There is the main altar at the front, My box to the right with my daughters Francoise and Petite Diane, the young Dauphin nearby (with his nurse). My daughter Louise, who is engaged, is with the Guises in an opposite box to the left of the altar.

Henri enters to polite applause. He wears a black coronation robe with our silver crescent moon motifs with some purple trims. He is anointed by the priests. The Archbishop conducts the service in Latin. He holds the crown of Charlemagne, which is big and bulky, over Henri's head before bestowing it upon him. He is given the 'hand of justice' and the orb. He stands up and turns around to shouts of 'Vive le Roi', 'Long live the King', 'Glory to the King'. He looks towards me at one point, grinning and gives me a wink with his glowing light brown eyes. I am so proud.

XXIV - Paris

As entrances stand, Diana's arrival, at the Ministry of Antiquities was memorable. It really wasn't Diana's fault. She had reserved an early train, she had arrived at the station in good time, to find that the train was delayed by an hour.

"I'm still OK," she said to herself.

She had allowed herself an extra two hours. What she had not factored in was the 'Mouvement des gilets Jaunes/Yellow Vest Movement's' blockade of the main rail termini and other transport infrastructure. Roads in and around Paris were in chaos. The taxi could only take her as far as Montmartre. Beyond that, she had to run. After a fifteen-minute run to the ministry, she was looking the worse for wear. Her smart business skirt suit was somewhat crumpled, she was out of breath, and her well-coiffured hair had turned into a hedgehog's nest of tangles and knots.

The Director of the ministry was at the reception when she arrived - on the dot of nine. He sniffed and looked her up and down.

"Ah, Doctor Garry. Professor Alain de Normandy, at your service." He smiled and reached out his hand.

"I'm very pleased to finally meet you in person Monsieur Director."

"Enchanté, please call me Alain. May I call you Diana?"

"Of course, you may, er, Alain."

The director leapt into his prepared spiel almost immediately.

"I have been following your progress at both Chenonceau and at Anet with keen interest. You have had remarkable success at both sites with great Roman finds - and those linked to our romantic past in the Renaissance. Remarkable!"

"Thank you, Alain," replied Diana, suitably flushed.

"It is for your success of the former, the temple to Diana or Artemis that I have brought you here today. But before I can go any further, I will require, if I may, for you to sign a non-disclosure agreement counter-signed by the president himself – my ultimate boss Monsieur Macron and his predecessors."

"Oh, wow. May I read it thoroughly before I do? asked Diana.

"Of course. Would you like a coffee?"

"Yes, please, black."

"But of course."

Diane read thoroughly and duly signed the NDA. More like the UK's Official Secrets Act, but it was necessary.

"Thank you," said the Director.

"The Pont D'Alma tunnel temple. It is not a myth." He blurted out.

"You are joking Monsieur Director. That was put out by conspiracy theorists after the death of Diana, Princess of Wales in 1997."

"Yes and no. Whatever the silly British Press think about the demise of their treasured princess is not of my concern. The reality of the antiquities is. And there is the ruin of the temple to Artemis / Diana, or perhaps otherwise Mithras under the basement of a building just across from the torch of liberty memorial by the Alma Bridge. Enough time has passed since that tragic event to allow us to carry on with our dig there. We would like you to take charge. Your Chancellor and Head of Department are amenable if you are?"

"Um, it is quite out of the blue, Director."

"Alain, please."

"OK. Will I have to give up Chenonceau?"

"Officially, no. Unofficially, yes. Though your deputy can cover for you while you are seconded here. You will be based in Paris - we have an apartment by the Louvre you can use. We will still pay for your rooms in Chenonceaux to allow you to visit. You have confidence in your Deputy, yes?"

"Yes, I do, Alain. It is a fantastic offer, but can I visit the site first before I decide. Also, will the finds ever be made public?"

"OK. Yes, and probably yes. The latter is sensitive, but not out of the question."

"Thank you. When would a visit be possible?"

"Would NOW be convenient?"

"Yes, I guess so. I have flat shoes in my bag."

"Don't worry Diana, access is quite good, your heels will be fine in the most part."

A car drew up outside of the building. It would seem that the blockade by the Yellow Vests had started to lift after the leaders were invited to see the ministers. The car was soon speeding towards the Pont D'Alma.

Diana and the Director exchanged pleasantries, but nothing was really discussed. Diana knew the mythos of the area. That the Kings of old in Celtic and post-Roman times had settled feuds by the banks of the Seine in that spot and that the body of the dead party would be carried away by the river. The river of souls. But how true that was, she could not say. The reality of a temple thrilled but also scared her somewhat. This was a great opportunity. What could she do?

After a long pause, Diana spoke again to the director.

“Alain, I would be happy to accept the post, but with some modifications to your suggestion.”

The director nodded.

“I would very much prefer a clean break from Chenonceau, and perhaps a ‘cover’ post here in Paris instead. And for my current assistant, Stan, to take over at Chenonceau. Perhaps he can be offered my current apartment or one of equivalent size. I could become ‘Head of Roman Temples in the Seine Area’ or similar, perhaps?”

“OK. He is young for that position, but it can be arranged. But you are happy to leave the dig at Chenonceau?”

“Yes, I think so. The time is right, and it will sort out a situation that could be a conflict between my personal feelings and my professional position.”

“I understand. We will make it so, Diana.”

XXV - Boxes

It was with some trepidation that Diana was found some two weeks later packing her books into boxes in her office in Chenonceau. Stan was helping her, while also shifting his things out of his office into what was about to be his new office.

"I'm still thrilled at my promotion, Diana, but I'll miss your steady hands and guidance."

"Thanks Stan. But you are ready, more than ready. And my new post is an advancement for me. But additionally, I won't be your boss anymore, so we're free to explore our personal feelings without conflict."

"I'm looking forward to that my love. And my new flat is yours any time you are over. Hopefully, on many weekends to come."

"I hope so. I'll enjoy coming back to Chenonceau, and to you. It really is my spiritual home."

A short while later a large van came to pick up Diana's belongings and take them to her new apartment and new life in Paris as Director of Roman Sites in Paris and the Seine Region. It was a perfect cover to allow the excavation of the Roman temple by the Pont D'Alma. The temple turned out to be dedicated to Diana but was co-sited with a temple to Mithras. Both the Sun and the Moon on one site.

The news of a real temple site was announced during a busy

week for news in the world. Nobody really noticed. It was billed as the temple to Mithras. Some conspiracy sites plus the 'Daily Express' in the UK picked up on it, but otherwise, it was sidelined by a crisis in the Middle East.

The dig at Chenonceau had also progressed in Diana's absence. The whole site of the temple had been uncovered in the corner of Diane's Garden. A greenhouse in the style of Kew Gardens had been temporarily erected carefully over the temple's form and had been chosen to be in keeping with the style of Diane's garden yet protect and display the temple with its precious mosaics. An ancillary pavement of deer grazing in the moonlight had been found in the antechamber. It complimented the beauty of the central Diana / Apollo mosaic uncovered while Diana Garry had been in charge.

As for the lovebirds, Diana and Stan - their romance now freed of the constriction of boss and co-worker had gone from strength to strength. Stan's visits to Paris and Diana's visits to Chenonceaux was something the couple looked forward to.

XXVI - Carcassonne

Well, it had started out as a romantic gesture, but fate had decided otherwise for Diana Garry and her boyfriend, Stan.

He had surprised her with a long weekend booking at a modest but comfortable hotel in Carcassonne as an early birthday present, but then he too had been surprised by a work commitment to visit the architects commissioned to build the permanent cover over Diane's garden at Chenonceau, so he had to cancel his part in the holiday.

It looked very much like Diana would be cancelling the whole booking until Tara popped up in Paris wanting Diana to show her around the sites. It appeared that yet another one of Tara's girlfriends had dumped her - this time on a city break in the French capital.

Not to be perturbed or ruin their potential time together it was promptly agreed that they would both travel down to Carcassonne by train the next morning and take in the sites. Diana had long been fascinated by the Cathars and desperately wanted to visit one of their leading sites. Beziers, the location of the massacre, had been another possibility but didn't have the same magic about it as the rebuilt citadel of Carcassonne.

Although criticised when it was first rebuilt by the architect Viollet-le-Duc in the mid-19th century, the alternative that had been previously proposed by the French government was to demolish it completely, since it had become so dilapidated.

In the end, the renovations were accepted and even feted by the locals, being granted UNESCO world heritage status in 1997.

Tara would not be so interested in the citadel as herself, but with some fine wine and food, she would have enjoyment enough.

Diana would have to put up with her sister's quirks, including being called 'Di', which nobody else called her, apart from her father.

Early the next morning Diana dropped round to her sister's budget Ibis hotel to meet up with her and go to the station with her. Tara didn't do mornings well but was putting a brave face on it.

"Hello, Di. I have had my breakfast and checked out. How far is it to the station?"

"Not far, Tara. We should be able to wheel our bags over to the station very easily. You do have a wheeled case, I presume?"

"Yes, of course. It's just here. Shall we head over?"

"Sure. We may have to make a stop-over in Toulouse, due to some engineering work on the line, but otherwise, it should be a good trip down."

Tara's snakeskin travel case clattered up the road along with her matching heels. Some things never changed.

Apart from her sexuality, Tara was very much her mother's daughter. A sharp contrast to Diana, who was wearing skinny jeans, a tasteful Parisian lace edged top and a leather jacket. She was her father's daughter. But despite all that, they were the closest of the siblings. Aphrodite barely spoke to them for months on end.

Diana was often heard consoling her sister after one girlfriend or another had jilted her. The joke was 'why not try a man?' when it happened, to which Tara always replied 'the worst girl is better than any man'. If the reverse ever happened, it was 'why not try a girl?' to which Diana said 'I prefer men, thanks'. Either way, they would both laugh and bemoan their ex.

At the station, Diana collected the tickets, and they waited on the station concourse for the platform to be announced.

"So, what's Stan like then Di?"

"He is the best. It's like we've known each other forever."

"That sounds serious. So not like the losers you usually date then?"

"I would not put it quite like that. But in terms of whether I see us together long term or not, I would have to say yes, instead of my usual no."

"I bet he's an only child."

"No, he has a sister, but I haven't seen any pictures of her, and he's been a bit vague about her."

"I guess I'll meet her at the wedding."

"Yes, if there ever were to be one. I'm not sure about Stan's commitment. At the end of the day, he is still a man and may not give me a ring."

"Oh, Di-di. I think he sounds great and would be mad to let you go."

"He is a fair bit younger than me. Suppose he finds a newer model?"

"No. I have a hunch not."

An announcement rang out from the speakers to confirm the platform for their train.

"Let's go, Tara. Platform 6. It is a replacement train since ours has a technical issue. We best get on and grab some seats as our booked seats are now invalid."

" Is there a buffet car? I could kill for a G and T."

"Unlikely, but knowing you, I presume you have a flask."

"Touché, my little sister."

Thankfully, the siblings found some reasonable seats and were able to sit down. The train was not quite as fast as they had hoped for, but the countryside looked pretty in the late Autumn sunshine. The conversation about Stan got more into the nitty-gritty, and Diana shared a few photos of her boyfriend with Tara.

"A goatee. Is Stan a hipster? I can just see his arse and pants poking out of his jeans."

"No, he's not! He's Czech, and over there intelligent people dress differently to those here. He has a certain amount of chic. I actually think you would approve. All of his trousers and jeans have proper belts."

"Hold on to this one Di. He seems like a keeper. What time did you say we get to Carcassonne?"

"Oh, shortly. In fact, I think I can spy the citadel in the near distance. But I do worry about those dark clouds. Surely it can't be snow?"

It was certainly colder than usual as they pulled into Carcassonne station.

The apartment turned out to be very near to the citadel itself and consequently far away from the train station. But Tara wanted to look at the shops rather than to take a taxi, so they walked through the narrow shopping streets of the town. They stopped at a natural make-up and fragrance shop where Diana treated herself to some purple nail varnish while Tara found a facemask to help rejuvenate her skin. A church was open to the road, and through it, a spectacular nativity scene could be seen, so the sisters popped in and took some photographs.

Further along, still Tara decided to invest in a jumper as the temperature was rapidly falling as the Sun was starting to set. It wasn't cheap, but it would keep her warm. It was a tasteful black in sharp contrast to her standard snakeskin or leopard skin patterns that she tended to favour.

The river crossing was a delightful scene. The old and modern bridges over the river were nicely lit in the late Autumn sunshine, as was the Citadel in the distance.

The siblings paused for a few pictures, including one of them taken together by a helpful passer-by. As the light was now distinctly fading, they carried on briskly to their apartment. Due to a misreading of the map, they took a few wrong turns before finding the apartment.

At the apartment, or rather, set of flats, the receptionist gave Diana the key and described how to get down to the block where their studio was.

Once through the door of the apartment, the sisters could appreciate how nice it was. It was on two levels, with a kitchenette, refrigerator, dining table and bed-settee on the lower level with a bathroom and bedroom on a higher level. The skylight of the top-level gave a view of the towers of the citadel towering nearby and above the road where the apartment was situated. It was agreed that Diana would take the upper bedroom so that she could chat to Stan and not disturb Tara.

They both took turns showering and changing into their evening wear ready to go out to one of the nearby restaurants in the old town.

A Tapas restaurant-bar serving French and Spanish dishes was recommended, and luckily a table was available for them when they went into it. The place was packed out with locals rather than tourists – always a good sign.

Tara suggested getting a red wine to go with the pork cheeks and herring dishes that they had initially chosen from the menu. The waiter recommended a local deep red wine, so they agreed to give it a try. It was indeed superb for its modest price. Deep and chocolatey, it went very well with the tapas dishes. The bread with olive oil and balsamic vinegar plus real French fries helped with the richness of the other plates. The atmosphere was completed by a local accordion player and the singing of many of the locals along to the tunes he played.

"So, Diana. What do you plan to do about bridesmaids?"

Diana was taken aback by her sister's forward question.

"Bridesmaids? I think you are a bit premature with that question. He hasn't asked me to marry him."

"Yet." Tara interrupted.

"OK, yet. And I really haven't thought about it. But I guess it would be you two plus Stan's sister. It's not as if I have any close friends really anyway. I have been married to my job for a long, long time."

"Oh, sweetie, that's great. I'll start looking at dresses."

"Well, OK. But if the style is outdated by the time Stan does pop the question, then please don't blame me. And no animal skins – not for a wedding – and if it does happen can you please ask Mummy not to wear black. She has so many other styles and colours, but it's always black at weddings. Aunty Madge and Viola didn't look too pleased with her at Viola's wedding. Although dad giving that extra speech was probably more memorable."

"Oh, Viola's face. It was an absolute picture. She was bright purple with embarrassment after his story about her as a kid."

"She was a right tomboy when she was a kid. I used to be scared to go over there to their house as I knew I'd get a bruise either from Viola or from climbing far higher than I was comfortable with."

"You weren't exactly the girliest girl back then though Di. The Vi versus Di show was the height of our Summer visit down to Torquay."

"I did nearly break my arm at least once."

"You mean again. You broke it at the Castle too."

"I won't exactly forget that, Tara. Did I get it right that you had a bit of a crush on her?"

"That was an evening to remember!"

"Gosh. Um, shall we order a dessert? All the travelling has given me a bit of an appetite."

"OK. Tarte au Tatin. I've not had it for ages, but it used to be my favourite."

"I don't think I've ever had it. I've heard of it, but never tasted it."

"You'll love it. With ice cream?"

"I shouldn't really. I'll not get my leggings on if I go too mad. You may need to finish it for me."

"OK. That's settled then."

Diana put in the order, and a few minutes later, they were enjoying a great piece of French cuisine.

"This is absolutely gorgeous, Di. What a good choice."

"Thanks. Can I ask you something, metaphysical?"

Tara's face gave a bit of a frown, before relaxing.

"I guess so. But you are the academic. I just dabble with Reiki and a little bit of Tarot. Though don't tell Mummy about the Tarot. She will probably think I have taken up Voodoo!"

"That's Mummy for sure. So, do you believe in reincarnation?"

"That's a deep question after a long day. In truth, I'm not sure. I did once sit in on a psychic development circle, and one or two of the ladies there made contact with 'spirit'. But I didn't."

"But do you think it's possible?"

"Yes, but why do you ask?"

"Well, on this set of excavations, I have experienced dreams and daydreams as if I were one of the people who lived at the dig sites."

"Wow, that's really cool. With your love of Roman temples that should be a great advantage to you with understanding what the artefacts are when you dig them up. Is it a he or a she? A Priest, Priestess or perhaps a Legionary?"

"Not Roman. She's a Duchess from the Renaissance era. And the dreams are vivid. I even feel, smell and taste some of the dreams."

"That's curious. But perfectly possible. It is said that we can live dozens of lifetimes. So I don't see why you shouldn't have been a Duchess. I presume she was French?"

"Yes, and the mistress of the King of France."

"Anyone I have heard of?"

"Diane de Poitiers."

"My grasp of Renaissance history is a bit poor. Did she ever meet Henry VIII or Anne Boleyn?"

"Well, actually, yes she did. She was a lady in waiting along with both Anne and Mary Boleyn and once met Henry VIII at Calais – or at least I met him in one of the dreams."

"Can you get his autograph?"

"What? No way. He was a tyrant and a womaniser. I don't think that Diane liked him."

"He was an uber bad boy, though. If you get the chance."

"I don't think it works like that. It's more like flashbacks. I don't wake up with coins in my hand or anything."

"No, I suppose not. This has been an evening of revelations. You would be the last person I'd have thought to bring up the topic of reincarnation."

"I know. A revelation to you. Much like you and Vi has been too."

The sisters laughed and drank some more of their wine. Both of them sat quietly in contemplation as the music continued for a while longer.

With their food finished, the wine drunk and the music ended, Diana asked for the bill. She offered to pay, but Tara offered to split it, so that was what they did. They left a generous tip and went, with waves from the remaining diners as they did so. Mainly from the men.

"Well, that was very nice. But I can't believe this snow."

"I know, not quite the South of France we were hoping for. The waiter said it was very unusual. Lucky us. Let's hope it warms up tomorrow."

"I think I'm ready for my bed now. I hope you won't be chatting to Stan into the early hours."

"I'll try not to. Stan has work to do, so it wouldn't be fair."

They walked back to the apartment. Before long Tara was asleep and Diana was in a deep conversation with Stan. In the early hours, she stopped and fell asleep.

The next day they awoke to a Sun high in the sky.

"Di, what time is it?"

"I don't know. I think my watch has stopped. According to that, it's around noon."

"That's what my mobile also says. Haven't we missed our breakfast?"

"Oh, no. It was from eight until ten. I wonder if we can persuade reception to let us have breakfast tomorrow instead?"

"Let's hope so."

"Shall we get up and drop into reception on the way out?"

"It looks pretty miserable and cold out. I don't fancy going out so far in that."

"Agreed, perhaps it will be better tomorrow, and we can tour the citadel properly then. But for now, I fancy a hot meal and perhaps a drink."

"Me too."

The receptionist was fully understanding and so moved their

breakfast booking to the following day.

They made their way up to the Citadel, sliding a little on the wet cobbles as they went. Tara's heels were not at all well suited to the walk-up. As it was so murky and moist, they unanimously agreed to go into a restaurant for a glass of mulled wine and a pot of the local game soup each.

They both laughed at their day so far.

"Welcome to the South of France Tara."

"Cannes in Summer next time babe."

"Yep."

"Still, nice mulled wine. No need to rush, I'm sure."

"I can't think of a reason. Besides, I think our gloves and shoes are still wet. I'll put them over by the fire."

"Thanks."

They mulled over their childhood while eating their lunch before heading off to look around the souvenir shops inside the Citadel walls. The narrow streets and high walls certainly gave this place an air of impregnability. The restoration had done an excellent job from what they could see.

They popped into a small café for a coffee before heading back down – carefully – to their apartment. The rain and sleet had eased off, and a mist had settled over parts of the old town. The tops of buildings poked out into the fog in places.

Once back inside, they changed out of their wet clothes and hung them up to dry.

"Shall we go to the same place again tonight? It was smashing last night."

"I could be persuaded. It looks like the best place in town. I just hope we can get in tonight."

"Me too."

They didn't. It was shut and locked up. Out of season most of the restaurants didn't open at weekends. But luckily another restaurant was open further up the slope. Inside the sparse furniture inside a space resembling a wine cellar gave the place a different atmosphere. With only a few other diners and no music, it was distinctly flat when compared to the restaurant-bar the night before. But with a menu of traditional Pays D'Oc fare they at least had the chance to try the native cuisine.

"I think I'll have the duck." Diana opened up the conversation.

"I fancy blue beef."

"What, the raw dish?"

"Not quite raw, but nearly. You tend to get a decent version in France. I don't think I'd bother back in the UK."

"OK, but don't have a bad tummy tomorrow."

"Promise, sis."

The dishes were both very well prepared, and both sisters enjoyed their meal. There was no tart option on the menu, so they both settled for chocolate mousse along with black coffee.

As they returned to the apartment, there was no snow tonight, so the walk along the pavement was a lot easier than the night before.

Stan was out for a formal dinner, so wasn't available for a chat, so after a brief conversation before bedtime, the sisters retired to bed.

The next morning the alarms went off at 8.00 am. They took turns for the shower and duly arrived at breakfast for 9.00 am. The croissants were freshly prepared, and the coffee was of good quality, so the breakfast was quite enjoyable. So much so that they decided to have breakfast before leaving the next morning as well.

After getting prepared with their cameras and warm jackets, the siblings made their way back up to the Citadel. The Sun was shining, so although it was cold, it was relatively pleasant. They decided to go straight into the inner keep of the Citadel. Diana had her purse out to pay for the tickets, but as it was the first Sunday of the new month, the entry was free. Luck was evidently on their side today, and perhaps the previous day's lie in had been for the best as the Sun really made the bastion walls shine in the clear air.

Once inside, Tara headed over to a signboard while for Diana, the sunshine faded in front of her eyes to show her a completely different scene.

One day I am out riding in the forest on sandy tracks with Louis. I am wearing a dark burgundy riding outfit of heavy suede for the chilly weather. It is overcast and gloomy but dry. I return to my home at Anet to hear of my father's arrest. Louis has to console me as I am so distraught with pain and anguish in my stomach. I discuss details at length with Louis over our meals. He is a friend of my father's.

I change into an oatmeal coloured heavy linen dress. Louis is in his heavy leathers and suedes for the autumnal weather. I am adamant. I will visit my father in prison. It is the case that Louis cannot risk being seen associating with Jean de Poitiers at this point. Instead, we decide that I will take the best and healthiest horse along with Louis' most trusted squire, Charles, to the prison, which is two days ride away from Anet.

We travel light with saddle packs. I wear a heavy green suede dress suited to the weather, and it is suitably low-key. We stay at coaching inns 'hotels' on the way. They are a bit basic and loud for me but are otherwise excellent. My appetite is even more miserable than usual. We stay in the outskirts of the prison town of Carcassonne then visit the prison first thing in the morning. The squire goes with me as far as he can. But I am on my own in the cell block.

The prison is very dark grey and forbidding. It is square with strong granite walls, rectangular, with regular blocks in its walls. It is not far from the castle keep. I speak to the prison governor – a big man, tall and thick-set. He warns me that it's not a place for a lady and he apologises. The gaoler leads me to the cell on the second floor. It smells of urine and worse. It is very unsanitary. The wide corridors allow full views end to end. My father is in a corner cell at the front. There is a deep, small window high up in the wall. There is sparse wooden furniture, including buckets – but he is also allowed to have a pen, ink, and paper (in case he confesses).

He looks ashen-faced, grey has aged markedly and is probably suffering from dysentery. He is overjoyed to see me. 'Papa!' I exclaim. 'My little Diane.' He replies. We embrace, and we both weep. After that, we both sit down on his bunk, and he tells me all that he can (in a quiet voice so as not to be overheard). I say that I will see the King, but my father is sure that the King's mind is made up. He asks me to look after my sister Mathilde. When the time comes, we embrace, and I leave.

Back at court, I request a private audience with the King (Francis I). He grants it. I wear a cream velvet dress with a black triangular wave pattern at the bottom of the skirt hem. I know that the King likes me in that. I approach him and curtsy low before he gestures me to get up. We discuss my father at length – I extoll his excellent service and that of his family to the Crown. Eventually, the King says he will think about it.

At Father's place of execution, he hears he is to be reprieved only after walking out to the executioner's block. It is cruel, but the King has insisted. I am overjoyed when I hear that he is not to be executed.

Diana resumed her ordinary consciousness seemingly without Tara noticing. Diana carried on with her tour and got a little bit carried away with photographing the views and examining the walls. Tara looked just a little bit bored by the end of their trip around the battlements.

"Shall we go for some lunch now, Tara. And maybe some mulled wine?"

"Do I!"

"OK, let's go. I'm a bit cold now, but this place is great. I'm so glad that they kept it."

"I'm surprised that so much of it is here. Wasn't this a Cathar stronghold that got captured by the crusaders?"

"Yes, that's correct. But the walls we see weren't around in the Cathar era. This is all later. It continued to be a vital stronghold for centuries afterwards."

"Oh, OK. I hadn't realised. My GCSE History didn't cover that. But I did learn a little about the Cathars. I used to imagine I was a Noblewoman in that era with a flowing gown and one of those conical hats with silk on them."

"The Bonne Homme – Good Men – as they called themselves were quite humble, so I'm not sure if they would have worn such elaborate clothing. But we don't know much about them as they were effectively wiped out. In modern terms, it was ethnic cleansing."

"Very sad."

"Yes."

At the restaurant, they again had hot mulled wine and a hot soup each before looking around the rest of the Citadel site, including the Cathedral. It had been derelict before it to had been rebuilt.

The evening was a repeat of the previous evening as the same restaurants were shut. But it was a pleasant meal with Tara having the duck and Diana eating a local artisan pork dish. The red wine was quite good, but not compared with that on the first evening.

Before they knew it, they were finishing their breakfast the next morning and preparing to check out.

"Can we get a taxi to the station this time."

"Yes, that's a good idea, Tara."

They checked out and waited a short while for the taxi to arrive.

When it arrived, they bundled their luggage in and set off for the station.

At the station, the scheduled train was running an hour late, and there was an earlier train imminently about the leave Diana went into her panic mode and wanted to jump on it. But Tara couldn't rush in her heels. So they ended up waiting for their original train. They went back out of the station and sat beside the Canal du Midi in the morning sunshine.

"Blue."

"What do you mean, blue, Tara?"

"Blue bridesmaids dresses. You will love them."

"I'm not so sure."

"Trust me."

The discussion carried on intermittently throughout the train journey until they arrived back in Paris.

Tara had to go off to the airport straight away, while Diana walked back to her flat. Her mind was on the Past and the Future.

XXVII - The Past

The apartment in the Louvre that Diana had been given in Paris actually turned out to be on the site of Diane de Poitiers' marriage to her husband Louis De Brézé, although none of that site remained.

It was on a visit in May just over a year after the couple got together that Stan dropped to one knee and proposed to Diana. She accepted immediately. The engagement ring was based on the design of the bracelet belonging to Diane de Poitiers – with crescent moon and inset with moldavite.

The date for the wedding was set for September the same year. The best surprise was that it was to be in the chapel of Chenonceau with the reception in the grounds of the château! The director of the château had given special permission to his honoured 'friends' as he put it.

With both of their tenures drawing to a close, it was great news that a new assignment was sent in their direction by the Head of Department of Bath Sulis University. A dig on mysterious possibly Roman, Phonecian or Greek ruins in the Bahamas. What a place for the honeymoon!

XXVIII - The Future

The wedding was spectacular. Diana's sisters Aphrodite and Tara were dressed in Renaissance/Pagan style bridesmaid's dresses of purple and accompanying amethyst jewellery. Tara seemed ill at ease with her full-length dress as she was so used to wearing jeans. At one point as she followed Diana up the aisle, she nearly tripped over in her dainty heeled sandals.

Diana herself wore a stunning full-length white gown with a classic boat neck, an antique lace veil - open - and flowing silk train embroidered at the edges with triple moon motifs 'borrowed' from Diane de Poitiers alternating between a combined S and D letter emblem. Her hair was styled up with a tiara woven in place. Her necklace had a magnificent blue fire emerald pendant upon it. Under her garment, she wore Diane de Poitiers' ankle bracelet on its replica leather mount – crescent moon and moldavite in place. That was borrowed for the wedding.

Stan wore a replica Renaissance hunting tunic in leather, complete with Huntsman's pouch. His beard looked slightly strange, being so well-trimmed. Stan's best man wore matching attire.

As Diana entered into the chapel, the guests gasped. She was initially led by her father (dressed in his usual faded grey suit and red jumper with a white shirt and tie). Halfway she left him and walked unaccompanied to the front to face Stan.

The priest, in traditional attire, gave a blessing in Latin before conducting the wedding service in both French and English. The vows were exchanged without any vow of obedience by Diana. She was and always would be a feminist of the most inclusive kind.

At the critical points, Stan's best man fumbled a little before producing both rings. They were bands of gold engraved with small hearts with secret engravings of 'D + S' on the inside of both matching rings.

With the service nearly over the bride, groom and witnesses went into an adjacent room to sign the register in front of the magistrate to make it all legal.

When the couple emerged, the chapel had emptied. The bride and groom were ushered up the stairs and out to the entrance where the guests, along with many tourists, were waiting to take photographs and throw dried petals of confetti (sanctioned for the occasion).

The wedding party then proceeded to a private suite within the restaurant outbuilding (a former stable) for the reception.

The wedding photographs taken with the backdrop of the Château of Chenonceau on a sunny day were beautiful. Diana shone in her elegant wedding dress with Stan's hunting outfit a great contrast. After a lady's hunting bow was handed to Diana, the scene seemed complete.

Stan's family were in attendance. His father had passed away a few years earlier, but his mother in her black gown cut a fine figure of elegance. His Sister Amelia towered over her mother. Diana later learned that she had been originally Stan's brother Zlot, but had transitioned a few years previously, and was now much happier, though living in Austria as the Czech border region with Poland was still a difficult place to live for transgender people.

The meal consisted of a buffet course of creamy chicken with boiled and roasted potatoes with the option of roasted peppers and vegetables for the vegetarians and vegans present.

After the main course, it was time for the speeches. First came Diana's father's address. It was hilarious, cringe-worthy, intellectually stimulating but also bumbling at the same time. He explained how during one of his many excavations at Corfe castle his youngest daughter, Diana, aged three, had climbed on an exposed wall ledge, then had tumbled into an excavated hole thus breaking her arm. She had been down there all night as her parents thought she had run away, Despite that incident, she had followed his own passion into archaeology, unlike her siblings.

Next came Stan's best man. He recounted how Stan had borrowed his uncle's fishing boat to get a better view of the annual festival fireworks in Prague. Heavy drinking had led him to attempt to take the boat back along the Vltava to her permanent berth. He failed. A short distance out he mistook the lights from a shoreside village like those of a cruise boat anchored in the river. Far too near the shore, he had struck an underwater reef and disabled the dinghy.

He had been lucky that he had slowed down by sobering up in the fresh air and by sighting water reeds poking out of the water's surface and lit up by a sizeable electric torch held up by one of the girls on the boat. The friends had all jumped into the chilly but shallow water to help drag the boat into the shore. There they anchored it below the cliff. They had all then been given a lift (Scooby-Doo style) by a farmer with a lantern in his old Russian all-terrain vehicle. That got them back to the city and Stan's Uncle's house.

His uncle was not best pleased but took Stan and his later best man to the river the next day to rescue the boat. From the top of the cliff, a small blue triangle appeared to be all that remained of the motorboat.

Stan's Uncle glared at Stan. They subsequently found that the actual dinghy was safely secured on the shore. It took a while to check the hull for leaks and re-secure the engine on to the transom. (Stan had tied the engine on well as it was worth much more than the boat). When the repairs were complete, they pushed the boat out into the river and set off. Stan's other friend, who had been staying with him from University, was bright red like a lobster from the Sun! Karma for persuading a drunken Stan to take the boat back along the river in the dark. Battles of Laski Riesling can be dangerous. The one Stan drank could have been lethal!

Next, Stan gave his speech. He recounted how he had first met Diana. Initially, she had seemed quite hostile and distant towards him until they discovered the joys of a mid-morning espresso and an afternoon cigarette break to discuss the dig and to get to know each other. The success at Chenonceau brought them together as if it were meant to be. The rest is history.

Lastly, in the new Feminist tradition, Diana gave her speech. She thanked her father and mother for raising her with a love of adventure and encouraging her to be confident. Diana said that she had always strived to be the best person she could be. Meeting a free spirit without pretensions was a breath of fresh air when she started working with Stan. Though her position as his boss had kept her aloof and distant from him for quite a while. Plus she thought he liked the younger girls. (Everyone laughed at that, except Stan who coughed as he was drinking his champagne at the time). She finished by saying that she felt she was the luckiest woman in the world.

The Best man proposed a toast to the bride and groom. The guests all lifted their glasses for the toast.

The polite conversations between guests along with the crème brulee and tarte au tatin pudding kept everyone occupied until the Ceilidh got started. Some Scottish heritage was being celebrated, though getting the band to Chenonceau was a costly treat and a logistical nightmare. As it was one of the fiddlers had got lost en route, so Diana's sister Aphrodite had stepped in to take his place, borrowing an older spare from another bandsman. Diana and Stan led the dances, though Stan's coordination wasn't that good, along with his unfamiliarity with the moves. But he tried.

Romance appeared to be in the air as Stan's sister and Diana's sister Tara were catching snogs between the dances. Diana's mother and other sister Aphrodite looked on disapprovingly.

After the Ceilidh there was a fruit and confectionery course to re-energise the guests before the disco. Again, Diana and Stan led the dance with one of Stan's favourite songs 'Romeo and Juliet' by Dire Straits. The next song was Diana's favourite 'Enjoy the Silence' by Depeche Mode. Amelia and Tara enjoyed every moment of those slow dances before scampering outside, giggling. Diana and Stan both chuckled.

At the end of the evening, Diana disappeared upstairs before reappearing in her Pagan/Renaissance style green full-length dress, ready to make her exit with Stan. Just before leaving, she threw her bouquet into the air. It was caught by Tara! It might be an exciting time ahead for the two families!

A horse-drawn carriage stood outside in the moonlight to take the couple up the long driveway up to the village of Chenonceaux where they were staying in the best bridal suite in town. The couple looked like a Hunter and Huntress in their Renaissance attire as they waved at the guests and ducked down as confetti petals were again thrown over their heads.

The wedding night would be full of final packing and preparation for the morning's flight to a new life in the Bahamas via Charles De Gaulle Airport and Orlando International.

The end?

Diana Garry will return in 'The Priestess'.

Fin

Epilogue

'there was an island situated in front of the straits which are by you called the Pillars of Heracles [Gibraltar]; the island was larger than Libya and Asia put together...this island of Atlantis'
Plato: Timaeus

How could a mythical island or its inhabitants have any bearing on archaeologist Diana Garry, now starting on an excavation around a partially submerged pile of rocks on the south side of South Bimini island in the Bahamas?

Afterword

I used writer's license with my usage of the term 'lunarium'!

I thought it would be a fun concept to introduce the idea that most temples to Diana or Artemis had a common feature that could easily be identified if you found its ruin.

The idea that a specific silver glazed tile had been used to create a crescent moon-shaped roof at one end of the temple that covered the altar and shimmered in the moonlight I found particularly appealing.

Acknowledgement

My thanks go out to Tiras Verey for producing such excellent cover graphics for this book and the others.

Thanks also need to go to Annie for her initial proofreading and that of my daughter Abby and other members of my family. I am sure that the final text is stronger for the checking.

Thanks also to Shari for not running a mile when I first contacted her some years ago and who has encouraged my ongoing interest in Diane de Poitiers.

Further Reading

‘A Portrait in Black and White’ by Shari Beck

‘The Serpent and The Moon’ by HRH Princess Michael of Kent

‘Madame Dupin: une féministe à Chenonceau au siècle des Lumières’ by Jean Buon and Michelle Perrot

About The Author

Amethyst Gray

Amethyst Gray was born on the Isle of Wight, England and grew up close to Carisbrooke Castle. The Island, Arthur C. Clarke's Mysterious World on TV, fossils on the beach and crystals gave her a keen interest in history, hidden history and how everything came about. She was always good at Mathematics, so she took a Physics degree at the University of London. That led to a career in IT before rediscovering her interest in crystals, alternative history and energy healing after moving to Wiltshire in the early 2010s.

Now, as well as being accomplished in IT, Amethyst teaches Angelic Reiki, practices Access Bars, Emotional Freedom Technique, Future Life Progression, and Past-Life Regression in the vicinity of Avebury stone circle.

She has given lectures on Atlantis, the water wizard Viktor Schauberger and the cloudbuster Wilhelm Reich. She is in the process of publishing her Diana Garry historical fantasy novel series. 'The Huntress' was released in August 2019, focussing upon Renaissance France, and 'The Priestess', based upon Atlantis, was published in March 2020. Finally, 'The Heiress' was published at the end of 2022 with insights into passengers of the Titanic disaster.

Additionally, she is collaborating with Steve Nicholls on 'The Little Book of Pyramids' series of books – 'The Little Book of Pyramids' (2020), 'The Little Book of Pyramid Meditation' (2020), 'The Little Book of Pyramid Intuition' (2021) and 'The Little Book of Pyramid Healing' (2022).

The Diana Garry Book Series

Diana Garry is a doctor of Archaeology at Bath Sulis University in the southwest of England.

In her 30s, she has long given up on the idea of romance in her life. However, she has one passion, and that is Archaeology. Diana has specialities in the Phoenicians, Celts and Romans.

The world is a clear and straightforward place, as is its history. Everybody knows and accepts that. Modern history started with the adoption of agriculture around 9000 BCE in the fertile crescent around the middle east that today includes northern Egypt, Israel, Jordan, Syria and Iraq. The ancient Sumerians, Babylonians, Assyrians, Egyptians, and Phoenicians were all responsible for developing civilisation as we know it.

People and events can be categorised as religious, irrational, logical, or scientific. Everything can be explained by science. Or so she thought.

In the Diana Garry book series, we follow Diana as her rigid belief systems are challenged in every possible way.

The Huntress

In 'The Huntress', Diana must confront her belief that reincarnation is a new-age idea gleaned from the far east without any basis on truth. She will glimpse the past, but not in an era she is comfortable with. And her relationships in her own life go in an unexpected but welcome direction.

The Priestess

In 'The Priestess', a more mature and happier Diana is brought in on a dig that always had the possibility of challenging Columbus or the Vikings as the first visitors to the Americas from the Old World. But its ultimate conclusions – about Atlantis - could challenge her more fundamental tenets. Will Diana get through this in one piece?

The Heiress

In 'The Heiress', a simple rescue dig finds a more relaxed and open-minded Diana once more being challenged. The history she knows and loves compared with the evidence and visions she sees in front of her as the ghosts of Titanic come to the surface.

Printed in Great Britain
by Amazon

58495445R00108